FALCONER'S JUDGEMENT

Ian Morson was born in Derby in 1947 and read modern languages at Oxford University. He now works in local government. *Falconer's Crusade*, his first novel to feature Regent Master William Falconer, is also available in Vista paperback. The third in the series, *Falconer and the Face of God*, is published by Gollancz in hardback. Ian Morson lives in Berkhamsted.

Also by Ian Morson in Vista

FALCONER'S CRUSADE

Ian Morson

Falconer's Judgement

First published in Great Britain 1995
by Victor Gollancz

This Vista edition published 1996
Vista is an imprint of the Cassell Group
Wellington House, 125 Strand, London WC2R 0BB

A catalogue record for this book is
available from the British Library.

ISBN 0 575 60004 7

Printed and bound in Great Britain by
Cox & Wyman Ltd, Reading, Berkshire.

96 97 98 99 10 9 8 7 6 5 4 3 2 1

Preface

Observant historians will know that the central event described in this story actually happened some years earlier than I place it. At that time Regent Master Falconer was not in Oxford. So I beg the indulgence of historians in making it possible for him to solve the mystery.

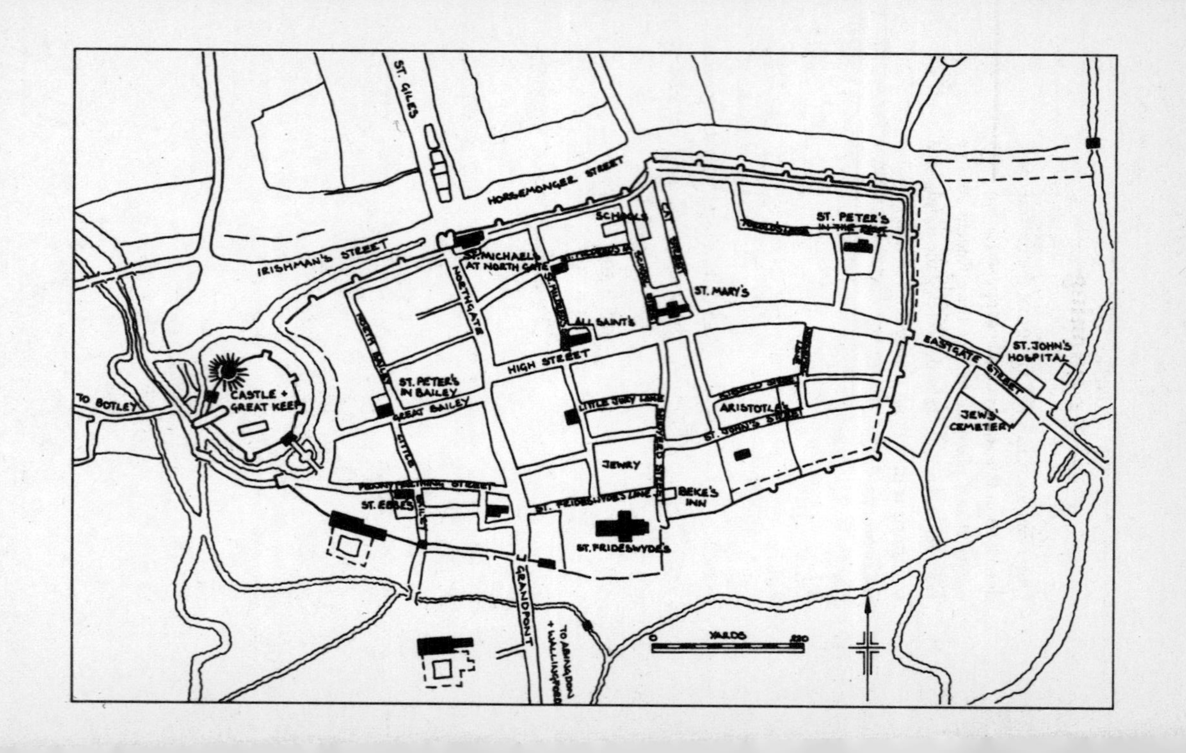

ST. GILES
HORSEMONGER STREET
IRISHMAN'S STREET
SCHOOLS
CAT STREET
ST. PETER'S IN THE EAST
ST. MICHAELS AT NORTH GATE
ST. MARY'S
NORTHGATE
ALL SAINTS
HIGH STREET
ST. JOHN'S HOSPITAL
EASTGATE STREET
ST. PETER'S IN BAILEY
GREAT BAILEY
CASTLE + GREAT KEEP
TO BOTLEY
LITTLE JURY LANE
ARISTOTLAL
ST. JOHN'S STREET
JEWS' CEMETERY
LITTLE
JEWRY
BEKE'S INN
ST. EBBES
ST. FRIDESWYDE'S
GRANDPONT
TO ABINGDON + WALLINGFORD
0 YARDS 220

The Beginning

In the beginning, God created the world without light or darkness. He created Heaven and the firmament, but we cannot see Heaven because of its height above the earth and the weakness of our eyes. For the first three days the world was in darkness. God then created the sun, moon and the stars, beasts and cattle, and before He rested on the seventh day He created Adam and Eve.

God set the sun in the East, where the equator is, and on the same day He made the moon and placed it in the East along with the bright stars. The sun outshines the moon and stars because it is Christ the Healer.

The first day of the world was March the eighteenth.

From the *Chronica Oseneiensis*

Prologue

The heavy scent of incense hung over the bedchamber like a miasmal fog that had risen off the River Tiber. The figure on the bed was draped in rich robes and his hands were clasped in silent prayer on his chest. Marble-faced, he seemed already to have metamorphosed into the icy statue that would soon top his tomb, without requiring the intervention of the stone-mason. In the far corner of the room a huddle of figures whispered urgently to each other, their heads close together as if afraid the figure on the bed would hear. One man turned his hooded eyes towards the bed, thinking he discerned movement, and almost craving the final stillness.

Seeing no evidence of the final act, the man turned back to those crowded around him. Although they were closely huddled together, the others seemed separated from him by an invisible barrier. His very presence demanded deference. When he spoke, all hung on his every word.

'I must speak with the Grand Master today. Arrange it, will you.'

The last words were spoken not as a request but a command. He pointed a beefy finger weighed down with rings at one of his hangers-on, who scurried out of the room to do his bidding.

'We cannot allow any other factions to gain a lead over us.'

All those around him knew that the 'other factions' came down to the Colonna family. No other groups were as powerful as the man's family, for he was an Orsini by birth.

'The Grand Master has intelligence agents everywhere between here and England, and if action is called for he will issue instructions to suit our purpose. The old fool is falling over himself to regain the favour of the Pope. This one or the next.'

The ring of richly garbed men around the speaker sniggered respectfully. But the man's attention was on the prostrate figure on the bed.

The sheets covering the dying man seemed so heavy as to press the life out of the frail figure. As if in protest at the group ignoring his struggle with the Angel of Death, he took a deep breath. The air snorted in through his angular nose, and the group of conspirators abruptly ceased their impromptu conclave. They hurried towards the bed, their heavy robes raising a cloud of dust from the floor. A myriad motes were transformed into sparkling jewels in the single shaft of Mediterranean sunlight that cut through the closed shutters into the darkened sickroom.

The leader of the group peered closely at the man's half-closed lids, but could discern no awareness in the eyes. He felt a soft breath on his face, and fancied he could smell the odour of cold earth on it. He looked back at the circle of faces around the bed, each with its own expression. Some were framed by fear, others by keen anticipation. Every one had good reason to wish to know the fate of the man on the bed.

Cardinal Benedetto gave the barest of negative movements of his head, and all concealed their feelings behind downcast eyes.

A slight figure stood alone at the foot of the bed as though barred from the circle of power around the dying man. He murmured a soft prayer of thanks for the life that continued to cling to the frail body on the bed. He had examined the man's urine that morning and there was no sign that he would die today, despite the apparent wishes of some of his colleagues. He set great store by the examination of urine as an indicator of the fate of the sick and felt a complicity with the man's hold on life. He resented the others in the group behaving as though the man was already gone, his power to be grasped and taken by another rather than dispensed by God. They even spoke of the campaign in

England in the most venal terms, mocking the sycophantic English King's efforts to buy favours for his family.

He lingered by the bed after the others had drifted back to their corner to continue their conspiracy. Thin and ascetic, he could not condone their greed, or the extraction of funds from remote parts of the Holy Roman Empire. The Church was too great to soil its hands with the coinage of bribery. He looked down at the figure on the bed, and saw more than a frail human body almost reduced to the skeleton it would soon be. He saw the long line of the man's predecessors linking the present with the early days of the Church and dreamed of himself carrying that holy torch forward. Master James of Troyes, Patriarch of Jerusalem, pulled himself up short – such thoughts made him no better than the others in the room.

Pope Alexander might be dying but while he lived he was still God's Vicar on Earth.

The First Seal

In the year 1239 that terrible race of inhuman souls known as the Tartars came swarming from the remote fastnesses of the East. They were as one with their steeds, never leaving their backs. To many they were the embodiment of the ancient centaur. Murdering all who stood in their way with sword and with bow and arrow, they laid waste to Hungary and its neighbouring lands. Thus is the First Seal broken. For it is written in Revelation that then a horseman with a bow came forth and rode out conquering the land.

From the *Chronica Oseneiensis*

Chapter One

The crowd filled the crossways at the bottom of the lane leading to Westminster Hall, the home of the King's Exchequer in London. Some knelt in the mud, their hands clasped in fearful entreaty to the Almighty. Others stood with their mouths agape, rooted to the earth as though in a trance. At the core of this silent knot of humanity, like a spider at the centre of his web, stood a Dominican friar, his hands raised to the heavens. His face was contorted with fervour, bulbous veins pulsating on the side of his head laid bare by the severe tonsure. He invoked the forgiveness of God for the palpable sins of those who stood around him, his voice piercing and lifting to the skies.

The fear gripping the crowd had come upon them because of the friar's words leading up to the prayer. He had assured them the Apocalypse was nigh.

'Did not your teachings warn you that the Sealed Book was fixed with seven seals? I have already told you of the consequences of the first five seals being broken. I am now here to tell you that at the breaking of the sixth seal, Revelation tells us that there would be earthquakes and the sun would turn black. All manner of storms would ravage the land.'

He paused and scanned the crowd.

'I need not remind you of the turmoil of the last years.'

His gaze pierced each and every person who stood in the crowd, as though his eyes could read to the depths of everyone's soul. And truly each person there was reminded of their own tragedy. It was only three years since, in 1258, a famine had ravaged England and one man recalled eating the bark off the trees to survive. In the year before that, another man's house had been swept away by floods caused by endless heavy rain. An older man, with a longer memory, remembered the year of 1252 when an unusually hot summer had claimed the lives of his grandparents, who died unable to draw breath. That same year a terrifying thunderstorm had raged on the day after the Assumption of the Blessed Virgin. Every person in the crowd provided his own natural disaster to fulfil the prophecy of the friar preacher.

His voice then broke into all their separate visions.

'At the breaking of the seventh seal you will all be judged and few will be called to paradise. The world will be rent asunder and there will be a new heaven and a new earth. The new Jerusalem will descend and God will have his dwelling on earth.'

He paused enough to give the crowd a crumb of hope, then dashed it from their hungry lips.

'But the cowards, the faithless, and the fornicators will burn for ever in the sulphurous lake.'

Now his prayerful invocation was stirring every soul to think of purifying his life before the impending Apocalypse. Every soul, that is, but the big, raw-boned man who stood at the periphery of the mob. William Falconer, Regent Master of the University of Oxford, was passing through London after his fruitless journey to Paris. Spying the crowd blocking the crossways, he had dismounted from the nag that was carrying him, albeit at a snail's pace, to Oxford and approached the throng with curiosity. He now regretted the waste of his time.

He had heard news of these apocalyptic visionaries, but this was his first encounter with one. He was not impressed. He thought the friar resembled a demented magpie pecking over the carrion remains. Indeed the man strutted round the patch of bare earth enclosed by the crowd exactly like the bird he so closely resembled.

Falconer snorted with laughter at the image he had conjured up in his mind. He turned to the man standing next to him at the back of the crowd, ready to pass on his amusement. All he saw in the man's eyes was a fixed stare of terror. It was as though the man had lost all volition of his own, and was given over entirely to the friar's message. Looking around him, Falconer realized most of the crowd was transfixed in a similar way. The only sounds were the echoes of the friar's prayer and the muted responses of the crowd.

Thoughtfully, Falconer turned back to his horse that stood neck bowed at the end of the rein he held in his left hand. He sighed. The hire of this animal and others had already cost him two shillings for the journey from Dover to London, and the remaining miles to Oxford would no doubt take him two more days and as much more money.

'Let us hope you can get me back to Oxford before the Apocalypse. I would like to be dressed in my best for the occasion.'

Not half a mile from where Falconer stood, the King of England, Henry III, was pondering seriously on his attire. Unusually, he was resident in London rather than away on one of his interminable journeys around his kingdom. The purpose of remaining in the capital was to speak to Bishop Otho, the Papal Legate, about preferment for members of the royal family. He had already gained the Kingdom of Sicily for his son Edmund – although there were two minor matters preventing him actually taking possession. The dying Pope had issued a bull withdrawing the gift and Manfred, the son of Frederick II, controlled the island and effectively stood in his way. However, the first was solved by Pope Alexander being on his deathbed. It only remained to wage a war in Sicily – and the nation would just have to pay for it. Henry shook his head in anger.

The servant who was draping his best surcoat over the stooping shoulders of the King backed away in horror at the tossed head. Had he somehow caused offence? Henry was a man of moderate stature, and of moderate habits, but he was still King of England. Seemingly oblivious to his servant's reaction the King strode off, shrugging the surcoat comfortably on to his narrow shoulders. His servant breathed a sigh of relief at being thus ignored.

Henry, concentrating on the coming audience with the Legate and eager to confirm matters with him before the Legate moved on to Oxford, almost missed the anxious voice that called after him down the corridor leading to the King's Chamber. However, he recognized the obsequious tones as those of one of his French kinsmen. He stopped and turned so abruptly the overweight figure of his half-brother, Aethelmar, almost collided with him. He was clad in the full regalia of his office as Archbishop of Winchester – another royal appointment that had filled the English clergy with ire.

'Your Majesty, I understand you are to speak with Bishop Otho.'

His red face betrayed his embarrassment and Henry realized he was on some errand for his powerful supporters in the realm. Why was he surrounded by vested interests and cliques, when all he sought was what was best for England? He had found lucrative appointments for his Lusignan relatives. To please the Queen he had given preferment to her family, although his barons had curtailed that recently and several hangers-on had been sent packing. And to please the Pope he constantly gave ecclesiastical benefices to Romans and other foreigners. When could he please himself? Now the Lord Archbishop danced from clumsy foot to clumsy foot in obvious anxiety over some further matter which would no doubt prevail upon his generosity.

The King stared coolly and expectantly at Aethelmar, the drooping lid of his left eye seeming to wink in complicity in whatever was afoot. The Archbishop laid open the plot that had been hatched by him and others that morning.

To the Frenchman, London was a welcome sight. Since seeing the ageing Grand Master of his order in Rome but a few weeks ago, he had been on the road ceaselessly. Crossing the snowy Alps had been exhilarating, especially the traverse of the Great St Bernard

Pass when his fingers had been stiff with frost and his breath hung from his lips like icicles. After that the endless plains of central France had simply been boring. But the crossing into England had tried his stoicism to the limit. The weather had seemed fair when he boarded the vessel at Wissant. But scarcely had they got out of sight of land, when a gale started blowing up the Channel. He pondered on the tales of crossings to England that had fatal results, and wished there was no body of water between England and France, so that he could have made the journey on horseback.

For days the vessel beat back and forth, making no headway at all. The grey churning sea had merged with the grey sky, filled with roiling clouds. At times he could not tell whether he was soaked by rain driving from the sky, or by waves breaking over the boat. Not that it mattered – both soaked and froze him to the bone. He tried to take his mind off the motion by cleaning his weapons of the salt that threatened to ruin them, but to no avail. The fragile little boat he travelled in had leapt and lurched from peak of wave to trough, like a dying stag seeking to shake out an arrow that had fatally pierced its side. Just when he had given up hope of ever seeing land again, the wind died and cracks of blue appeared in the blanket of cloud.

The crew of the vessel were encouraged to raise more sail, and looked visibly more relaxed. It was an English ship, and the sailors who had been too busy to engage him in conversation during the storm now cheerily asked him what his business was in England. But he was suspicious of who was an innocent and who a spy, and did not offer any response. Long and bitter experience had taught him not to trust anyone. Soon his cold and silent nature put the sailors off, and they ignored him for the rest of the trip. On reaching their harbour, they had rejoiced openly in his discomfort when, sick as a dog, he vomited his last meal over the side of the boat. It was ironic that he had not felt ill during the whole storm, and in a flat calm had succumbed. But Guillaume de Beaujeu acknowledged he was no sailor – his talents lay elsewhere.

He had hoped for a short rest once he was on shore at Dover. But he had been met by a sergeant of his order, and they had chased the scudding clouds of the disappearing storm out of the port. A string of horses had carried them without a stop through Canterbury and Rochester to the outskirts of London. Now at least he could present his credentials to the local master of the commanderie in London, and explain the wishes of the master of them both. He bore orders given direct to him by the hand of the Grand Master of the Knights of the Temple of Solomon.

The Papal Legate was dyspeptic and out of sorts, and it was going to affect his meeting with the King. He had summoned his new doctor and the man had prescribed a medicine he was even now preparing. Bishop Otho belched loudly, the taste of the previous day's fish returning to his tongue, sour and metallic. He went to the door and was about to call impatiently for the doctor, when he saw him in conversation through an open door at the opposite end of the passage. He called the man, his English name unfamiliar on his tongue.

'Hanyball, hurry now. The King is waiting for me.'

The doctor, a new recruit to the Legate's retinue in England, scurried up the passage, a pewter cup in his hands. The Bishop snatched it from him, and was about to swallow the decoction in one draught when he saw the look of apprehension in the man's eyes. Otho slowly lowered the cup from his lips, and sniffed its contents. The apprehension in the doctor's eyes turned to stark fear, and he made to leave. But before Hanyball could escape, Otho wrapped his beefy arm around the man's throat and tipped his head back.

'Drink it yourself.'

The doctor's eyes almost popped out of his head and sweat trickled down his cheeks. He grunted and shook his head wildly. Otho pressed his fat fingers around the man's mouth, forcing his teeth apart. The doctor's gurgling protest was drowned in the drug pouring over his lips and down his chest. He coughed and some of the liquid shot out from between his teeth. Otho persevered, ensuring that at least some was swallowed despite every effort by the other man. Defeated, the doctor went limp and the Bishop released him from his stranglehold. Hanyball fell to his knees on the cold flagstones, his whole frame shuddering. In vain he tried to force his fingers down his own throat to vomit up the decoction. Before he could raise his hand to his lips, he lost control over his movements, tumbling backwards and cracking his head on the ground. His legs thrashed for a few seconds and a great gasp escaped his lips, then he lay still.

Bishop Otho stood over the body and rearranged his robes. He could not keep the English King waiting any longer, despite the attempt on his life. He would need to speak with his bodyguard about this later. Who had instigated the act? Who had the doctor been speaking to through the doorway, before Otho had summoned him? Silently he cursed his impetuosity which had resulted in the man's death. So much better to have kept him alive and tortured the truth from him. But first to see what Henry wanted.

The banquet proved to be a tedious affair for the Bishop, and inconclusive in uncovering the mind of King Henry. It was relieved only by one amusing event towards the end. First he and the King had been led to silver bowls of water, where they had washed their hands. At this point there had been too many servants hovering around for Otho to make any overtures, and it would have been unseemly to turn to business so soon. They were led to the table, placed high on a dais overlooking the other participants in the feast, all of them no doubt sycophants at the court of the King.

As each course was brought, the King's steward touched the King's portion with what he claimed to be the horn of a unicorn. This was supposed to protect the King from poisoning. Otho preferred the ministrations of his master of cooks, Sinibaldo, who was his own personal protection from such attempts on his life. Sinibaldo had supervised the preparation of the meal, and now hovered close behind his chair. Otho recalled the incident before his audience with the King, and resolved that Sinibaldo taste his medicine too.

After the soup came endless English stews, which were no different to Otho's palate from the soup that had gone before. Indeed, every course tasted of the same herbs and spices. This monotony was relieved only by the cooked heron that the King himself insisted on ritually carving – to the murmured approbation of his retinue. After the meats came various subtleties, including something the King referred to as a flathon. It pleased Otho and he asked Sinibaldo to discover its making. He later learned it was a simple custard made with milk and yolk of eggs and that rarest of commodities, sugar. This was poured into a pastry shape the English called a coffin. Sinibaldo's tasting made sure there was no prophecy in the shape. The final course was a range of confections made in the shape of beasts, each with the King's coat of arms on it.

Throughout the meal, Henry avoided any direct commitment to supporting Otho in his quest for the Papacy. Otho was becoming a little annoyed with the King, though he dare not show it. It therefore gave him pleasure when the King was discomfited by his jester. It happened this way. Throughout the meal various jongleurs had wandered in and out of the tables, but the King's own jester with his shaven head and parti-coloured jerkin had caused the most amusement. Flushed with his success, he approached the high table at the end of the banquet and spoke out loud.

'Hear you, my masters. Our King is like unto our Lord Jesus Christ.'

The King, proud of his own piety, was flattered, and replied. 'How so?'

'Because our Lord was as wise at the moment of his birth as

when he was thirty years old. Likewise our King is as wise now as he was when a little child.'

The jester cackled and shook his stick of bells at the King. He was the only one who laughed. Slowly a murmur of conversation filled the embarrassed void, and Otho smirked behind his beefy hand. Unfortunately, the King took it badly and rose from the table and left the hall, leaving behind a white-faced and trembling jester. The Bishop then realized he had lost the chance to pin the King down, and rued his own pleasure at Henry's discomfiture.

Humphrey Segrim knelt in the shadows cast by one of the great stone pillars supporting the arch of St Frideswide's Church. Outside, a rumble of thunder marked the gathering storm that threatened to break the oppressive heat of the day now ending. Inside, Segrim prayed that the storm clouds would keep any worshippers away. Oxford was a nest of idle gossip and he did not want to be seen speaking to the cleric he awaited. His head was bowed, his face cupped in his soft, white hands in the attitude of pious communion with his God. His thoughts, however, were elsewhere. As the cold stone flags struck through the cloth at his knees, he cursed the man's tardiness.

He raised his head up and gazed at the image over the altar. He uttered a silent prayer to the Almighty for the success of his enterprise. The future of his family fortunes rested in his hands. And that of his co-conspirator, who was late for his appointment. Then the slapping sound of leather on stone, echoing through the empty church, caused him to look round. Silhouetted against the weak and watery sun, shining through the open door to the nave, was the approaching figure of a cleric, his hood pulled over his head. Segrim squirmed to ease the ache in his knees and buried his face in his hands once again. He was aware the man had knelt by his side, and heard a murmured prayer. The voice, when it came, was strong and seemed to ring around the church.

'I believe I can be of service.'

'Yes, but keep your voice down.'

'There is only the Lord to hear, and I have no secrets from Him.'

Segrim didn't doubt the cleric's sincerity. After all, that was why he was being used – in what he thought of as the Lord's work. He quickly explained the plan concerning Bishop Otho, who was due to arrive in Oxford in a day or two and would be sojourning in Oseney Abbey outside the walls of the city. The man listened intently as Segrim explained what it was necessary to do. Finally he produced what he saw as the crowning argument.

'The King himself is concerned that this should come about. So I insist – the man must be killed and quickly.'

Chapter Two

It had taken William Falconer fully two days to reach Oxford. Much of the route was churned to mud, due to unseasonably wet weather. And towards the end of his journey, he had deferred to a faster moving retinue of horses and wagons belonging, he later learned, to the Papal Legate on his way to the same destination. After the passing of the vast household, the roadway was left rutted and muddy, slowing even more the funereal pace of his own hired nag.

He was at least safely home now, one month after leaving to look for Roger Bacon in Paris. He had resolved to find his old friend who had been spirited away from Oxford four years earlier by the Franciscan brotherhood to which he belonged. In that time a few scraps of second-hand information had come Falconer's way, brought by travellers and scholars from across the Channel. He was worried about what was being done to Bacon in the name of the Church. And the stories he was told lived up to his greatest fears. It was said that Bacon was denied any opportunity to carry on writing, indeed that he was forbidden access to any books and scientific instruments. Falconer feared this would all but kill his friend. He had warned him that the Church would not tolerate his views being so openly expressed, and that the Friar General would be forced to act. But Bacon was too engrossed in the search for knowledge to understand the workings of smaller minds – to his own misfortune.

Then, just three months ago, Falconer had been passed a scrap of paper by an itinerant jongleur. It bore the unmistakable script of his friend Roger Bacon. He read it eagerly but the cryptic note, obviously penned in haste, merely directed him to Brucius de

Valle, a scholar at the University of Paris. Thus his last month had been spent in a hopeful trip to France, only to find that de Valle had no knowledge of the whereabouts of Roger Bacon. He explained he had merely been passed some papers by another scholar, who himself had known Bacon during his residency at the university.

These papers now lay in a scattered heap in front of Falconer. He was strangely hesitant to unfold them, as though they were some sacred text. Indeed he had spent the whole sorry trip back from France reluctant to examine the untidy bundle of papers, some with Bacon's own hand visible on their surface. Now the time had come to act, but still he first sat back from the table and scanned the chamber in which he sat, lit by the flickering flame of a tallow candle. His room in Aristotle's Hall was of sufficient size to contain his experiments, but afforded little space for his own comforts. To the left of the chimney breast was a toppling stack of his most cherished books and papers, where standard church works such as the *Historia Scholastica* were lost and buried under more used and well-thumbed texts of the Arab mathematician Al-Khowarizmi, medical works, and studies of geography such as *De Sphaera Mundi*. To the right of the fireplace were several jars of various sizes, some of which exuded strange aromas. Although Falconer no longer noticed this, they were the first thing most of his visitors commented on – much to his surprise. In one corner stood his bed, with a small chest at the foot of it – the repository of his worldly possessions. The centre of the room was occupied by a massive oaken table on which was piled a jumble of items, each of some significance in Falconer's scientific searchings. There were animal bones, human skulls, small jars of spices, carved wooden figures, bundles of dried herbs, stones that glittered, and lumps of rock sheared off to reveal strange shapes inside their depths. But now the table seemed dominated by the pile of papers formerly belonging to Friar Roger Bacon, known as 'Doctor Admirabilis'.

Falconer had waited until the night had come, so that he would not be disturbed by the clerk-students in his care at Aristotle's Hall. Anyway it seemed strangely appropriate to open the bundle in the dead of night. Friar Bacon had pored over his own experiments mostly at night, by the light of an uncertain candle. He also did it to avoid disturbance, but had merely earned himself the reputation of a necromancer. Now Falconer was faced with the magician's treasure. With trembling hands, he unfastened the dirty ribbon that bound the pile of papers together and began to sift the documents. Many were pieces of paper torn from larger documents, with writing squeezed over every inch of the surface – mute testimony to Bacon's deprivation.

The first scrap that attracted his attention was covered with astronomical calculations. It predicted phases of the moon and movements of the sun, with specific times, days and hours for eclipses of those heavenly bodies. Falconer carefully set that to one side, noting that one eclipse prediction was for a few weeks hence. The next item that came to hand was a brief treatise on the power of words, in which Bacon asserted that there existed a means to compel others to act against their will in a kind of waking trance. He declared he had seen this used with certain esoteric passes of the hand and soothing words. Falconer was sceptical of this, but out of respect for his old friend he reserved his judgement. How he wished Bacon were still here so that he could discourse on such matters with the friar.

As he worked through the other papers he sorted them into mathematical treatises, alchemical works and notes on metaphysics. He hoped that one day Bacon would be allowed to expand on his theories and record them fully for other scholars. The thought that he held all that would be left of the man's compendious mind for future generations filled him with horror, not least because he knew he would not fully understand all that was written on the papers in front of him.

He lifted up one sheet of paper that was covered with writing.

He had been fascinated at first sight by what was contained in it, but delayed giving it his close attention until he had sorted all the rest. Now he scanned what was written on it again in more detail.

It was full of remarkable predictions, including one that Falconer attributed to wishful thinking, bearing in mind the friar's predicament. For he described an instrument 'of the height and breadth of three fingers' which could raise and lower weights immeasurably greater than itself. Thus, he explained, a man might free himself from prison by raising and lowering himself from a tower. Falconer was more taken by the description of conveyances. Bacon asserted that wagons might be made to move at incalculable speeds without the motive power of animals. That ships of unimaginable size might be made to move without sail or oar at the control of one man alone. And, more exciting for Falconer than all these, that a flying instrument might be made whereby a man, sitting in the middle of the machine, might beat with wings and fly like a bird. The friar believed all these things had been done of old, although he was unsure of the flying machine. This one notion had fired Falconer to endless experiment since Bacon had first carelessly mentioned it in conversation. To fly like a bird: Falconer could scarcely restrain the conjecture that sprung up in his imagination.

At that moment, there was a flurry of sound at the window arch, and through the opening as if in mockery of Falconer's thoughts hopped a barn owl, white and ghostly in the guttering candle flame.

'Ah, Balthazar. Good hunting?' questioned the Regent Master of his companion. The owl merely hopped on to his perch in the corner of the room and returned Falconer's stare with his disconcertingly human eyes. He was the best of companions for the Regent Master, all-knowing and unerringly terse in his responses to questioning. Falconer crossed tiredly to the open window arch and stared up at the blood-red moon. Perhaps Roger Bacon at this moment was staring at it too.

* * *

Someone much closer to William Falconer than Roger Bacon was gazing at the same moon. Bishop Otho, the Papal Legate to England, was pacing the bedchamber of his rooms in Oseney Abbey. The abbey stood in the middle of the water-meadows a half-mile to the west of Oxford, its yellowed stone walls like a reflection of those of the town. Narrow channels of water criss-crossed the meadows, and bone-chilling mists rose from their turgid surfaces. What ill-luck to be in this cold, wet land, remote from the Mediterranean warmth of Rome, at such a time. Remote too from the vultures hovering over His Holiness's bed. He should be in Rome promoting his cause as the successor to Alexander IV. In his absence he did not doubt that his rivals were already canvassing the cardinals. Guy de Foulques would be seeking support with large bribes and liberal promises of preferment. He almost howled at the moon in frustration, his bulbous nose pointed to the sky like the muzzle of a Roman wolf.

A soft knock at the door of his bedchamber revealed he had disturbed his secretary in the next room. The man never seemed to sleep and annoyed the Bishop with his fawning concern for the needs of his master. Otho sighed.

'Yes, Boniface.'

The Savoyard poked his thin, pinched face around the door, an obsequious look on his face.

'Forgive me, Holiness. I thought I heard a noise.' He sniggered. 'I could swear it was the howl of a wolf. Are there such creatures in these parts?'

Bishop Otho realized he must have indeed given voice to his frustrations, and forced himself to appear unconcerned. Relaxing for almost the first time since the attempt upon his life in London, he sank into the cushioned chair next to the fireplace. Despite the obnoxious nature of his secretary, he found him useful as a sounding board and explained his worries. Boniface nodded eagerly.

'And yet, it may serve us well, being in England. King Henry is so anxious to please the Pope, whoever he may be, that I am sure he will support your candidature for the Papal Throne. He appears to be more than willing to bleed his people dry of money for anything that promotes the position of his family in the world. Or satisfies his finer religious feelings.'

He turned his weasel face to the Bishop, who sat slumped in the chair by the pale ashes of his bedchamber fire. The Bishop was clearly already imagining the papal crown on his brow. His eyes were staring into the far distance to a future he yearned to hold firm in his grasp. He recalled the copy of Henry's general letter to all abbots and priors in the counties of England that he had personally delivered to the Abbot of Oseney. He had been present when Henry had dictated it and recalled the phrases that rolled off the King's lips. Henry reminded the religious fraternity that they should 'do honour to their prince, under whose protective wing they breathed freely'. Reminding them of his need to 'incur considerable expense in the cause of the Crusades', he humbly requested their help in meeting such expenses. Such a request could not be ignored, and much-needed coinage would flow into the channels of bribery that were required to make a pope.

If only Otho could be sure that it would be used to promote his own cause. He had not been able to see the King again after the incident at the banquet. Still, the King had been most flattering before the idiot jester spoiled things, and people said Henry was incapable of duplicity. Even if that avenue failed him, as Legate he was in a position to require a procuration of dues to the Pope from all abbots and bishops. He could demand at least four marks from each and every ecclesiastical establishment in the land, and take the first coin for himself. It would not be the first time such an action had been taken. That would serve to swell his bribery funds. A satisfied smile broke across his florid features and he rubbed his fat hands together.

'Excellent. I feel a small celebration is in order. Tell Sinibaldo to prepare something special for me for tomorrow's meal.'

The Bishop's secretary bowed and scurried from the room to pass on his master's wishes to the Legate's master of cooks.

The night was proving long and hard for the Frenchman. It was two days since Guillaume de Beaujeu had presented his credentials to the master of the commanderie in London. Although he could not reveal his true purpose, he knew the papers had included a message from the Grand Master, and he had expected a level of respect that was not being offered. The master had claimed he had a matter of discipline on his mind, but that he would address the Frenchman's needs for funds and a horse as soon as possible. In the meantime, he was left fuming at the delay. He had resolved to force the issue this evening, after his shared meal with the brother knights in the Temple commanderie. But barely had he finished the simple repast that was offered him in the kitchens, than the master demanded he and the others be present in the Templar church.

He followed the other knights who were stationed in the commanderie across the stone courtyard, the sound of their feet strangely deadened by the darkness. They were guided by a stream of yellow light that poured out of the main doors of the church across the cobbled yard.

The church was circular in reflection of the Holy Sepulchre in Jerusalem, and the interior was crowned by the large domed ceiling raised on tiers of squat pillars around its circumference. The centre of the bare floor was dominated by a stark and forbidding central altar. Although many torches blazed from braziers high on the walls, the pillars threw deep shadows, which shifted back and forth in the unsteady light. A stone seat ran round the whole outer edge of the edifice and the knights, tight-lipped, took their places in this gloomy vault. The Frenchman was one of the last to be seated and almost immediately the chaplain scurried to the central altar, his gloved hands clutching an ornate cross. His droning voice drifted up with the smoke from the torches to a grey fog that obscured the apex of the dome. The newly arrived Templar's tired eyes began to droop.

He was awoken by an angry buzz from the lips of the other knights. In the entrance to the church stood two burly sergeants of the order with a hunched bundle between them. The bundle was a man who could barely stand. The sergeants had to support him as they dragged him forward. The Frenchman realized he must have been shut up in the commanderie prison for some time. The cell was a box barely four feet in each of its dimensions. The pain of not being able to stretch was excruciating, and resulted in a man being unable to support himself. He wondered what the man had done.

The master of the commanderie stepped forward, his shadow cast like a cloak over the figure of the prisoner. The unfortunate wretch had to kneel at the feet of his commander as he was accused of fornicating with another man in the common dormitory. The Frenchman shuddered at the thought of the deed and the punishment to come. He suddenly realized his name was being called.

'Guillaume de Beaujeu, please step forward.'

Wearily, the Frenchman stood, knowing he could not refuse the command. His reputation preceded him, and sometimes it was a nuisance. He crossed the cold stone floor aware that every eye in the church was upon him. Pushing aside the dagger that was offered him by the master, he paused in front of the kneeling figure. The poor wretch stared up with fear-filled eyes at de Beaujeu, who whispered a brief prayer in his native French and crossed himself. He then leaned close to the condemned man and spoke softly in his ear, like a lover whispering endearments. This seemed to calm the other man, and once again de Beaujeu felt a sense of communion between this, his next victim, and himself.

He slipped round behind the kneeling figure, drawing a silken cord from his robe as he did so. With an expert flick of his wrists the cord was around the man's neck and his powerful hands administered the Silent Death he had learned in the Holy Lands.

* * *

Ralph Harbottle, the Abbot of Oseney, was a man of uncommon piety. He liked to run the affairs of the abbey with an eye for firm monastic discipline. That is not to say he was an ascetic. The abbey was, after all, wealthy and continued to earn significant incomes from the buildings in its possession in the streets of Oxford, outside the walls of which the abbey stood. No, Ralph believed in strict monastic order – an enthusiasm unusual in these times – but he still shared in the fruits of the abbey's riches. To satisfy his conscience, he left all those secular matters to his bursar, Brother Peter Talam. The man frightened the Abbot with his severe nature and constant invocation of the Lord in all his doings. He avoided Brother Peter when he could, and felt inadequate in his presence despite having travelled to Rome to see the Pope.

He far preferred the companionship of his prior, John Darby, who took care of all the claustral affairs for the Abbot. Brother John was the antithesis of Brother Peter. They were of the same height, but where the bursar was thin and brooding, with dark eyes that seemed to suck your very soul from your body, the prior was chubby and rubicund. The one was cold and mannered in his actions, the other cheerful and given to indiscretion. The Abbot wondered, not for the first time, that their roles were an apparent reversal of their natures. He might have thought the bursar more inclined to matters of claustral discipline, and the prior more at home in the kitchen and the collection of rents.

However, Peter Talam managed the external affairs of the abbey with scrupulous attention to detail. Nor did he seek to profit himself from the transactions he carried out, as many a less honest monk was inclined to do. As for John Darby, it was his pleasure to keep the chronicles of the abbey. He spent much time chattering with visitors and the other monks, relying on his open nature to encourage frankness. When he was not exchanging opinions with someone, he spent most of his time in the Scriptorium, carefully recording events as they unfolded in the wider world. And more importantly for the Abbot, recording the history of the abbey itself. Ralph hoped he occupied a favourable place in the chronicles. One day, he would summon the courage to ask to see his prior's writings. In the meantime, he would ensure the man had nothing adverse to record about him.

This very thought brought him back to the matter that had kept him awake most of the previous night. The presence in Oseney Abbey of the Papal Legate confronted him with a dilemma. The man was too powerful to offend, but the realization that before he left he would press for a significant part of the abbey's wealth filled Ralph with dread. It was not in his nature to dispossess the abbey of any of its assets. Perhaps he could arrange for the Bishop to see Brother Peter. He would not wish to wager on the outcome of a match between those two.

Both Brother Peter and Brother John were already busy that damp and cloudy morning. After matins and lauds they went about their duties while their lesser brethren contemplated the day in the chapter house, which for some meant dozing until dawn rose. Neither monk was aware of the other's activity as their cells were on different floors of the abbey. Brother John had arranged for living quarters near to the Scriptorium, which was located high on the southern face of the abbey. This lofty perch ensured that the brothers occupied with the copying of manuscripts could work until the sun almost dropped below the horizon. From dawn till dusk the large arched windows gathered in the natural light and ensured a long and profitable day for the copyists. John Darby worked on an elevated podium next to the largest window from where he supervised the brothers and was able to make best use himself of the sun's rays.

Today did not bode well for natural light, however, and John contemplated the expense of lighted candles, which would no doubt be needed for part of the day. He stood at his window looking south across the River Thames at the wooded land which bordered that side of Oxford. From where he stood he could not see the town, and indeed his thoughts were less of it and more of the King and his capital city which lay off to the east.

Peter Talam's view, from his ground-floor cell, was precisely of the town which furnished much of the income for the abbey. His damp and gloomy room symbolized not only his denial of any worldly comforts, but reminded him constantly of how the abbey retained its powerful position. He would be occupied today with collecting rents and arranging the purchase of provisions to replace those used up by the massive consumption of the Papal Legate and his retinue. He was contemptuous of the excesses of the Lord Bishop, whose sybaritic indulgence was betrayed on his florid, puffed-up features. Brother Peter consoled himself with the thought that if the plans he had worked, then he would shortly not need to worry about the man.

William Falconer awoke with an ache in his neck. He was sprawled across the table that stood in the centre of his room, and the friar's papers lay scattered around him. He had obviously dozed off at some early hour of the morning, his mind crammed with a bewildering array of concepts. Most of all, he recalled the instrument for human flight described by his friend. He cautiously raised his head and winced as a stab of pain shot into his shoulders. The room was cold and damp, his clothes clinging to him as though he had slept in the rain. He rued once again the strategic reason for the location of the town. The fact that it had been possible to ford the Thames at this point may have been good cause to locate a settlement here, but the marshy nature of the low-lying land meant that even the summers in Oxford were dank affairs, plagued with insects. March would soon be sliding into April and any daytime warmth served only to raise heavy mists from the boggy land surrounding the town. On windless days this curtain hemmed in the noxious humours of the daily life of the more than two thousand souls who inhabited Oxford.

The town itself was now long established as a university town first and foremost. The traders resented the primacy of the University, but lived from servicing the learned community. William

Falconer was only one of many Regent Masters who taught the Seven Liberal Arts of antiquity. The foundation for all students was the Trivium – Grammar, Rhetoric and Logic. After that, and of greater importance at Oxford than other centres of learning such as Paris, the edifice of knowledge was raised with the Quadrivium – Music, Arithmetic, Geometry and Astronomy. Four years of study would lead to a Bachelor's degree in Arts. But this had to be followed by another three years of study, reading and disputing, before the scholar could call himself a Master. He was then under some obligation to teach others, but many left a year or two later for lucrative ecclesiastical posts. Although this meant there was a large body of young men teaching at the University, some were of more mature years. Falconer ruefully put himself in this category. Many of his contemporaries were travelling the long road that led to Doctor of Medicine or Divinity – a journey of twenty years staying in one place.

Falconer's own youth had been spent on more active journeys across the world, lengthening his route even to the humble level of teaching Master. The further labour of a Doctorate was not for him now. Now he satisfied himself with a personal approach to study, and was content to teach the endless procession of youths who passed through his hall, Aristotle's by name. His income from the hall was supplemented by a meagre benefice from the owners of Aristotle's, to whom he paid rent. Like many houses and inns in Oxford, Aristotle's Hall was owned by Abbot Ralph of Oseney Abbey.

Falconer knew that today he must visit the abbey and pay his long overdue rent. If he did not do so, then the pittance the Abbot gave him to support his teaching would not be forthcoming. And Falconer needed it for the bare necessities of his life. Putting aside further consideration of Friar Bacon's texts, he blew on the cinders in his grate and roused the embers of the fire to something that would dry his damp robes. He did not relish the thought of negotiating what was his by right from the hands of the bursar at the abbey. The man was parsimonious and self-righteous also, an intolerable combination for Falconer. Perhaps he could put off the evil deed until after dinner. He had, after all, a duty to his students first. Pleased to have justified a delay until the early afternoon, Falconer began to gather together the valuable store of knowledge on his table. He would deposit it safely in the chest at the foot of his bed, where it would lie on the top of his best gown and surcoat, clothes he rarely had occasion to wear.

As he shuffled the documents, his eyes fell on the treatise on the waking trance and he sank down on to the stool beside his fireplace. As his clothes gently steamed he once again read through Bacon's assertion of the strange technique, wondering if it could be possible. He sat oblivious to the encroaching light as the day that was to prove so fateful to many and fatal to one in particular reluctantly dawned.

The Second Seal

In the year 1244 a great battle was fought between the Christians and Khorazmians near Gaza. It happened on the 12th of December, on the vigil of the Feast of St Lucy. Many Christians, along with the whole army of the King of Syria, were obliterated by the Khorazmian horde. In this way was the Second Seal broken, and we still see the effect in England now with the ruled fighting against the ruler. For Revelation says that when the Second Seal was broken another horse appeared, its rider having the power to take peace from the earth and cause men to murder one another.

From the *Chronica Oseneiensis*

Chapter Three

Guillaume de Beaujeu had travelled through the night to reach his destination, and saw the sun rise from horseback. The last few days had been exhausting for him, but he showed little of it on his stoic features. His order demanded poverty, chastity and obedience, and he found at least the first simple to observe. He had little desire to own material things when his order would furnish all he needed. It also pleased him to give his life obediently to the order. However, he sometimes followed his own instincts, rather than obeying slavishly the instructions of the Grand Master. But he could discipline himself to be obedient, especially when he was instructed to play the intricate games of chess with people at which he was so adept. The notion of chastity was most difficult for him to contain, especially when he found himself surrounded by desirable forms. He thought of the gross deeds of the knight he had recently despatched, and grimaced. In the end, sublimation of his own desires became merely another game he played with himself.

He stirred in his saddle, the leather creaking under him, and he spurred his horse across the sturdy bridge over the Thames. The road was the main southern approach to Oxford, and the soft stone walls of the city glowed like gold in the watery morning sun. He turned his head to the west, and could just make out Oseney Abbey, a squat shape catching the light on its own outer walls. Momentarily, the sun sparkled off a window in the distant building and the Templar squinted. The purpose of his trip across that damned Channel slumbered in those buildings, but there was plenty of time to plan the game in hand. His first step was to find the Golden Cross Inn at Oxford and take a room. Then he would contact the Bishop's master of cooks and carry out his task. The inn belonged to Oseney Abbey and it would be a fine irony for him to achieve his goal from there.

As the morning progressed Bishop Otho was well pleased with what he achieved. Admittedly, it could have started poorly due to his audience with the Abbot's bursar. The man had proved particularly obstinate in his insistence on knowing the specific uses to which the monies demanded were to be put. The Bishop was used to fawning and obsequious monks, and pompous and blustering abbots. He had never encountered a man both unimpressed by his position and yet so apparently willing to comply once his questions had been answered. Otho was ultimately forced to admire the man, and reckoned he would be eminently suited to the political intrigues of the Curia in Rome. Both knew the abbey would have to bow to the wishes of the King and Pope. Both knew a game was being played to save face. It had been a truly Roman duel, which the Bishop relished. In the best traditions of Rome, the interruption of good food left the matter unresolved. For the Papal Legate nothing was more important than an excellent repast, and he was anticipating the best from his master of cooks.

It had proved to be so, thanks to the fact that the Bishop travelled with his own cooks from Rome. This meant he was not subject, in his own residence at least, to the awful stews that the English prepared with spices drowning out the flavour of the meat, and fruits boiled down to liquids fit only for feeding toothless old men. This afternoon he dined on the most delicate *pollo* from the abbey's own farm, flavoured with basil and cooked in olive oil from the jars that travelled everywhere with the Legate.

As he settled on his couch, the aroma of the meal seemed to waft again under his nose. He half opened his drooping eyelids, and saw his master of cooks hovering at the door. The man's large frame filled the doorway and he appeared uncertain whether to enter or not, unaware the Bishop had seen him. Otho spoke sleepily.

'Sinibaldo, what do you want? Either come in and speak, or leave. But don't hover.'

Sinibaldo wrung his fat hands, and opened his mouth to say something. Then clearly changed his mind, shaking his head.

'Oh, it's nothing. I just wanted to be sure your meal was satisfactory.'

As the man retreated from the entrance, the Bishop muttered his approbation.

'Indeed it was. Indeed it was.'

His mouth almost watered anew at the recollection as he settled his gross frame on the couch for a short sleep. Later he would have the burdensome task of being polite to some local dignitaries.

Falconer's meal had been a much simpler repast of cheese and ale. Now he could no longer put off the business of confronting Brother Talam. Leaving his young charges to study by themselves, he turned down the narrow lanes running by the south walls of the town. The path was awash with the filth thrown carelessly out of the houses that overhung the lanes. And the damp heat of the afternoon turned the turbid liquid into an air-borne humour that seemed to cling to Falconer's clothes. Turning the lane at Corner Hall, he was glad to pass the grounds of St Frideswide's Church where the sweet scent of wildflowers cut through the stench. He left the town by the small postern gate in the west wall which stood under the looming St George's Tower. Breathing the less fetid air of the open meadows, Falconer followed the muddy track leading to the abbey. The imposing cluster of buildings stood on a small rise in the middle of the flood-prone fields, and access was by one path running over several rivulets that ran down into the Thames.

Crossing the rickety footbridge over Trill Mill stream, he came upon the tail of a crowd of cheerfully noisy students, clearly also making their way to the abbey. It was not until he was close to the rear of the rowdy throng that he recognized any of them, and knew them for some of the poorer clerks. Despite the apparently piercing nature of his blue eyes, which he used to bore into the conscience of many a guilty clerk, Falconer's sight was increasingly poor. He relied on his wits to conceal his incapacity, knowing how cruel jests would be made about it and the bird for which he was named. He simply rued the years he had spent poring over texts in candlelight, to which he attributed the ruination of his sight.

Knowing some of the clerks at the rear of the crowd by name, he hailed them and fell alongside one, engaging him in conversation.

'It's William Coksale, isn't it?'

The youth nodded.

'And why are you and your friends off to the abbey, when you should be studying for your Responsions?'

The gentle chiding caused Coksale to blush.

'It is what happens after our passing of examinations that concerns us. Most of us do not have wealthy patrons, and must find benefices by making connections where we can.'

'Especially when the King prefers foreigners over native-born Englishmen?'

Coksale left his concurrence unsaid, for everyone knew that despite the actions of the influential barons over the last year or two, the King was unrepentant in his support for the Pope's appointees to the English Church. The Papal Legate himself had bestowed many vacant benefices on his own retinue the minute he had set foot in England.

'We thought we would pay our respects to Bishop Otho and hope to win some favours in return. We understand he is most amenable after the dinner hour.'

The last was said with a knowing smile, obviously directed at Falconer. The youth clearly thought Falconer was also seeking preferment, but the Master soon corrected the mistaken impression.

'I fear my business is not with the Lord Bishop, and is about more mundane matters.'

He patted the empty purse fastened to his belt, and bid farewell to William Coksale. The crowd split respectfully as he strode through them, and he nodded at some faces he recognized. Most were cheerful, but some were grim-faced, as though their future depended on this day – as well it could. One young man, accoutred with a bow and set of arrows, seemed glassy-eyed with fear of what was to come. Falconer recalled seeing a similar stare in someone else's eyes recently, but could not remember whom. Putting it out of his mind, he strode under the arch of the abbey gate, passing with some embarrassment the outstretched hand of an indigent priest who hovered at the entrance. By his accent he took him for an Irishman, and wished him better luck at his begging with the Abbot or the Bishop. It would have been impossible for him to give anyway, as he had no money.

As the man made off towards the cloisters, Falconer was glad to feel the faint cool breeze that the buildings trapped on humid days such as today. It served to confirm the well-organized nature of monastic life in comparison to the chaos of communal life in Oxford. He paused to let the welcome breeze wash across his face. The recent storm had not abated the sullen heat of the day, which now caused his heavy robes to stick to him. As he leaned against the chapel wall, he let the cool of the stone strike through his damp clothes.

'Master Falconer.'

The sharp tones of the monk's voice cut through Falconer's pleasure. He opened his eyes to be confronted with his Nemesis in the shape of a tall, grim-faced monk, the hood of his habit thrown back.

'Brother Peter. I have been looking forward to our meeting.'

The monk's silence said that either he did not believe Falconer, or if he did the feeling was not a mutual one.

'Follow me.'

As he turned to lead Falconer to his quarters, both men saw the crowd of students approaching the archway to the main courtyard of the abbey. Before them stood the squat shape of a man at ease with his powerful frame. The monk grimaced.

'If they have come to see the Papal Legate, they will not get past him.'

'Who is he?' Falconer asked curiously.

'The Bishop's bodyguard. There has been more than one attempt on his life recently, and it is as difficult to see him as the Pope himself. Unless you have money or influence. The Bishop is currently in audience with some people with money. Probably too much money, for I would imagine they wish to lavish it upon the Bishop in return for favours. He is unlikely to interrupt that for a ragged rabble of penniless students.'

The last words were spoken with distaste, and the monk beckoned Falconer down a cool, dark passage away from the potential confrontation.

Bearing in mind what then took place, Falconer was to regret not seeing what transpired himself. It was always so difficult to garner the truth from a motley crew of unreliable witnesses after the event. However, follow the monk he did and was agreeably pleased that Brother Peter seemed anxious to conclude their business quickly. Falconer always found his room and his company depressing. So he was glad when the bursar swiftly counted out his stipend, deducting the year's rent, and excused himself on the pretext of more important business.

Falconer decided to use the time available to him to speak with John Darby, whom he found altogether more amenable. The monk was supervising the copying of some texts of Aristotle for the Regent Master. Falconer had obtained an authentic Greek text about natural science through his friend Jehozadok, a Jewish priest in the town. Previously, Aristotle had been known only through commentaries on Arabic texts translated from the Syriac, itself translated from the Greek – not a course guaranteed to open Aristotle's true thoughts to the Western world.

On entering the Scriptorium, Falconer was disappointed not to see the friendly, rosy-cheeked face at the raised desk at the end of the room. Two rows of pale-faced monks sat on high stools painstakingly copying texts for the abbey library and the atmosphere was of intense concentration. The burnished wooden desks were scattered with papers, and each had a horn box filled with quills. Each copyist worked to his own rhythms, scanning text, inking his quill and writing. There was a constant scratching sound, like grasshoppers in high summer, as many quill points travelled over paper leaving their trail of knowledge. Each monk's head rose and dipped as he read the original he was copying and returned to the copy. Tonsured heads bobbed in a matching rhythm to the pens.

Light still streamed in from the high windows, although the afternoon was well advanced. The nearest copyist to the door raised his head from his task after a few minutes and looked enquiringly at Falconer. The Master knew him for one of the monks entrusted with the task of copying Aristotle. However, he knew better than to ask if the youth had any opinions of the text. He had been chosen by John Darby not only because of his accuracy and beautiful hand, but because of his total ignorance of the content of any text he copied. The Church did not approve of Aristotle's views on the sciences, and none of its elite could be tarnished by the concepts. In this context the young monk, accurate and uncomprehending, was perfect for the task.

'Brother John is not here, I see.'

The young man silently shook his head and held his quill poised ready to return to his work. Politely but firmly dismissed, Falconer left the monks to their task. As he began to descend the creaky wooden stairs that led down from the Scriptorium, he heard a great shout in the courtyard below. Turning back up the stairs, he re-entered the Scriptorium to find the reverse of the calm room he had left moments ago. Stools were scattered on the floor, and the normally sedate monks who occupied them were struggling at the windows to see whatever was afoot. The view was obscured by well-padded backsides in heavy woollen habits, and anyway Falconer's eyes were too feeble for a distant aspect. So, knowing he was unlikely to learn much from this vantage point, he retraced his steps down the staircase, leaping two or three steps at a time.

In the courtyard all was chaos. A large group of students was beating upon the vast oak door that led to the guest hall. The thunder of their fists echoed around the normally calm abbey. In the middle of the open yard lay the bloodied shape of the Legate's bodyguard. At first Falconer thought he was dead. But even as he screwed up his eyes to see better, the man groaned and rolled over. Falconer breathed a sigh of relief and turned his attention to the conflict in hand. To his right he could see another group of the students entering the cloisters, clearly intent on finding another entry to the Bishop's quarters. As they began to stream around the sheltered arcade, a cry came from several.

'There he is. Thief of our money!'

'Thief of our livings!'

There was a flash of purple and gold as the Bishop, still in his canonical cope, left the far end of the cloisters and was hustled by his servants to the abbey church. The group of students at the oaken door gave up their efforts to break it down, and responded to the cries. One student had found a blazing torch and had applied it to the door in an attempt to burn it down. A long smear of black disfigured the heavily studded surface and the brand lay smouldering on the stone step. The knot of angry youths now followed on the heels of their comrades in a pincer movement down both sides of the cloisters. The cries of the students were like baying hounds pursuing their prey.

Falconer was left wondering what could have sparked such extreme action. Whatever it was, the outcome would be equally extreme for the whole of Oxford. He stepped out of the archway that had hidden him from the mob and immediately bumped into a hurrying figure. Both men clutched at each other, as though expecting the other to land a blow. Falconer was the quicker to react and pinioned the other's arms at his side. He was confronted with the angry, red face of the abbey's prior, Brother John Darby. His normally rubicund features were distorted and he took a few seconds to recover his calm and catch his breath. Imagining that the monk had been on his way to render the Bishop some assistance, Falconer offered his help and went to follow where the mob of students had gone. But the monk held him by the sleeve, and pulled him in the opposite direction back towards the guest hall.

'Follow me. The Bishop will be safe in the church, and if necessary he can wait until dark to make his escape. There is something more urgent for us to deal with.'

He saw the puzzlement on Falconer's face.

'There's been a murder. I need your help.'

Brother John led Falconer through a side door to the guest hall that the student mob had not seen. He followed along a corridor that led up to the inside of the same massive oak door the students had been beating on. From this side there was no sign of damage and a sturdy metal bolt suggested the mob had had no chance of entering this way. To one side of the entrance hall there was an archway that led to the kitchens. The monk scurried through the arch, and the scene that greeted Falconer was one of chaos. Several heavy pans were overturned and a swill of food was smeared across the floor. Two petrified servants stood pressed against the far wall as though they wished to pass through it and disappear. Their eyes were agog with fear and fixed on the floor. In the centre of the room, face-down on the cold, grey flagstones, lay a body with an arrow piercing the centre of its back. Over the body knelt an ashen-faced Peter Talam.

'Brother Bursar!' exclaimed Darby. 'What are you doing here?'

Talam rose quickly to his feet.

'I was waiting in the ante-room to see the Bishop. What on earth has happened?'

Falconer pushed aside the two monks and began to examine the scene. The man's face, pressed to the floor, was turned towards Falconer and he could see a trickle of blood running from the corner of his mouth to mingle with the spoiled meal that lay around him. Careless of the food on the floor, Falconer knelt by the body and examined the wound. The arrow had pierced the back at an acute upwards angle and was buried deep in the flesh. It must have entered the heart and the man would probably have been dead as he hit the floor.

His eyes were still open and a look of shock was written on his face. The man was large, and his face red and heavily jowled. One cheek was squashed against the cold floor, and his mouth was half-open revealing yellowed teeth. His bulbous nose filled the centre of his florid face. One podgy hand was flung out as though to break his fall. The other arm was crushed at an odd angle under his body. Falconer stood up, wiping the stain of food from his shabby robe, and examined the position of the body again.

From where he stood he could look through the archway of the kitchen and clearly see the oaken door that was the main entrance to the Bishop's quarters. The head of the dead man was pointed towards the archway.

'Has anyone moved the body?'

The two cooks stared at each other in incomprehension and Brother John responded first.

'I was here before them and that was how he lay. These two were busy closing the main door on the students and only came through after I called them.'

He pointed with an ink-stained finger at the body.

'He was already dead, of course.'

'And the arrow was fired from outside?'

'Obviously. One of your students is guilty of murder. You must find him and punish him.'

Falconer merely grunted and turned to the two cooks.

'Did you see the arrow fired?'

Both men looked puzzled, until Falconer gestured at the arrow still protruding from the body. In an accent heavy with inflections of Rome, the older of the two explained he did not see who fired the arrow, but that it narrowly missed him as he strove to push the door closed. The other nodded vigorously in agreement. However, neither knew what had caused the riot in the first place. Nor had either one seen the arrow actually hit the man now slumped on the floor. Or at least they were not saying if they had, relying on their poor command of the language to protect them.

'Does it matter if they did see?' asked the prior impatiently. 'It clearly did hit him. The evidence is before your eyes.'

'Undoubtedly,' replied Falconer, his tones calming the agitated monk. 'I am simply applying Aristotle's deductive logic to the situation. This requires the establishment of general truths not open to reasonable doubt. Then, when you put them together, they often imply a further truth not previously seen, which can then be demonstrated.'

'Now is not the time for a lecture.'

'Perhaps. It is certainly not the time either to question a group of hot-heads intent on causing the Bishop harm. They will give up shortly, if your confidence in the security of the church is to be trusted. Tomorrow will be soon enough.'

Brother John was about to object, when there came a thunderous knocking on the door. Both cooks looked nervously at the monks and their inquisitor. Falconer could not believe that it would be the students returned to cause more mischief. The sole target of their anger was ensconced in the abbey church, and they would not be politely knocking to gain admittance there. He gestured for the Bishop's servants to let in whoever it was. With reluctance they pulled back the heavy bolt and swung the door open. Outside, and quite alone, stood a squat man leaning on a large but rusty sword. A crooked smile crossed his leathery face as he spotted the Regent Master.

'I might have known you would be here.'

'Hello, Peter.'

He gestured for the man to come in and introduced him to the monks.

'If you have not encountered him before, Brother John, this ugly brute is Peter Bullock, the town's constable, and a good friend of mine.'

Bullock and Falconer might have seemed unlikely comrades-in-arms. The constable served the burghers of the town, who paid him to take on their responsibilities of maintaining the law. His demeanour betrayed him as an old foot soldier of simple origins. Despite his bent back and age, adversaries found him bewilderingly quick in turning situations to his advantage. He was a man of physical courage and even temperament. Falconer, the Regent Master and philosopher of the University, should have lived in a different world to the constable. But Falconer's curiosity on matters of strange deaths had thrown them together, and the Master had soon found need of the other's skills. It looked as though they might be needed again.

'I understand there has been a little disturbance here. Caused by some of your students,' Bullock began.

Falconer shook his head sadly.

'I fear it is more than a little disturbance.'

He stepped aside and revealed the disorder in the kitchen. Bullock's eyes focused on the body in the centre of the room. He quietly cursed and stepped up to it.

'Who is he?'

Brother Peter supplied the information.

'He's called Sinibaldo. He is . . . was the Bishop's master of cooks.'

Bullock's curses redoubled and he wiped his huge fist across his face. He turned to Falconer.

'I hope you are not going to get yourself involved in this matter, my friend. This is not just a scrap between some students and town traders. This is high politics.'

'What? The killing of a cook?'

Bullock looked down at the rich, multi-coloured robes that adorned the large frame of the man lying dead on the floor – robes now ruined with his blood.

'I think he was more than a mere cook, William. Even I can deduce that, without the benefit of Aristotle.'

He was in perpetual disagreement with Falconer's strange methodology. He could not accept that some obscure philosophy was able to identify a murderer. His methods had more to do with seeking reasons for guilt, reasons such as revenge or envy. But he had to admit that the Regent Master was more often right than wrong, however he arrived at his conclusions.

'No, this will have to go further than you or I, my friend.'

Falconer merely shook his head.

'There is nothing to prevent us seeking our own truths, whatever ripples this all causes in the wider world.'

He scanned the room again and his eyes fell on something he had not spotted before. He pushed past the two frightened cooks and ran his fingers along a deep, fresh gash in the wooden frame of the doorway that led to the scullery.

'Don't you see? There is something very wrong here.'

'Indeed there is, and I am about to put it right.'

The harsh and heavy voice caused everyone in the room to turn from Falconer. In the archway stood a tall and opulently caparisoned man of full years. Peter Bullock knew him to be Humphrey Segrim, a landowner and burgher of great influence in the town. The man's face was contorted with rage.

'I have already sent my servant to Abingdon, for I know the King is in residence and would wish to protect the Lord Bishop from this student rabble. His soldiers will no doubt be here soon.'

He gestured towards the body.

'I now see there is more than just the gross offence to the Bishop to charge the mob with. This will be grave for the whole University.'

There was a ring of pleasure in his words.

Chapter Four

It was market day in Oxford, and even the untimely death of the Legate's master of cooks could not stop that. For days traders had been making their way towards the market town and only when they reached Oxford did most of them hear of the murder. In many of the taverns there was little sympathy expressed for the foreigner. There were too many of them in England anyway. Although the market was not the attraction it was twenty years ago, it was still a riotous throng of merchants, each set on selling their own produce. And today the good weather had ensured a full attendance of sellers and buyers. The confusion even started outside the city walls. The main road leading down towards North Gate was the traditional site for the sale of cattle and sheep. This morning, as every market morning, woven hurdles strove to keep one farmer's animals from another's. Sometimes they failed and red-faced farm boys scurried round and round, slapping cows' haunches with hazel twigs in an effort to control them. Burly farmers stood face to face arguing over whose sheep was whose. The miasma of dung and steaming animals hung over the whole incoherent mass.

Any traveller who penetrated this press of livestock and entered Oxford at North Gate was confronted with a human melee. The narrow lane which led to the junction with the High Street was lined with stalls. On each were laid out the horticultural efforts of the region. Every trader vied with his neighbour to attract attention by calling out his prices louder than the other.

Turning east along the High Street, the traveller would find the more established trades. In shops no more than six feet wide, spicer competed with spicer and goldsmith with goldsmith in the same part of the town. In the back of many shops, a craftsman sat bent over a table hammering and shaping his wares, which were laid out at the front for the passer-by to admire. Today their trade was subdued, and they blamed the friar.

At the widest part of the street, a great crowd had gathered, turning their backs on the shops. They all faced inwards towards a single figure, who stood with his hands raised to the heavens. He wore the robes of a Dominican friar, stained with recent travel. His face was contorted with emotion, and the bright morning sun seemed to create a halo round his severely tonsured head. He held the crowd with his words, which echoed off the walls of St Mary's Church, in front of which he stood. The church was soon to be rebuilt and the crumbling façade seemed to reflect the friar's exposition on the collapse of society.

'Your lives are like this market. They are full of people, and adorned with a great paraphernalia of trinkets. But after the market has gone, the alleys of your lives are left strewn with more filth than ever before.'

The murmur from the crowd confirmed for the friar that he had the onlookers' attention. He went on to his main thesis.

'You must repent now, for the days of the Last Judgement are on us. The Bible prophesies what is to happen at the breaking of the Seven Seals. You have only to look into your past to see the time is come.'

As with the crowds he had addressed in London, he led these gullible people to reflect on any disaster that had occurred to them over the years and to attribute it to the coming Apocalypse. Today he had another example to convince them of impending doom – and to serve the political aims of his order, which had no time for the Roman establishment.

'Only yesterday an agent of the Anti-Christ was struck down by the hand of God. One of the Pope's servants, sent to oppress us, was justly killed. For it is written that at the breaking of the Seventh Seal all the beasts of Satan will be laid low.'

At the front of the crowd, as at other assemblies, several men fell to their knees ignoring the noisome stew that ran down the middle of the street. On market day the sewage channel ran stronger and more putrid. But the souls who knelt by it were oblivious to anything but their own salvation. They hung on every word that the friar spoke and awaited his absolution. The words that followed would have been familiar to William Falconer, for he had heard them from the same lips in London but a few days earlier.

'At the breaking of the Seventh Seal you will all be judged but few will be called to paradise. The world will be ripped asunder and there will be a new heaven and a new earth. The new Jerusalem will descend and God will have his dwelling on this earth. But the cowards, the faithless, and the fornicators will burn for ever in the sulphurous pit.'

Many in the assembled throng wept.

Thomas de Cantilupe was not yet officially the Chancellor of the University of Oxford. But he had already been nominated by the Bishop of Lincoln to replace the old man who had effectively ceased to carry out his duties. De Cantilupe was an ambitious man, and he saw this appointment as a stepping-stone to greater preferment. So he was anxious that nothing should go wrong so soon. He could imagine the criticisms – not yet Chancellor and the students are already out of control. He therefore took the unusual step of involving the town authorities in the rounding up of the students who had caused yesterday's affray. Earlier that morning Peter Bullock had stood before de Cantilupe, in as upright a stance as his bent back permitted him. He had listened as the Chancellor-to-be rambled on about the events of the previous day.

'Once the King had been alerted to the straits the Bishop was in, he sent soldiers to rescue him. Thank goodness, they were able to cross the Thames with the Bishop under cover of darkness and escort him to Abingdon.'

Bullock had heard that the Bishop had tumbled off his horse in the middle of fording the river, and had been dragged by the collar of his canonical robes to the southern bank. There, he had been unceremoniously dumped in the cow pasture whilst his horse was retrieved. The stench that stuck to him had ensured his escort kept at a respectful distance thereafter. The thought brought a smile to Bullock's lips, which de Cantilupe interpreted as approval of the saving of the Papal Legate. He continued his diatribe.

'Naturally the King was outraged at the offence shown to the Lord Bishop and wishes the culprits caught. Especially the killer of his master of cooks. It will not bode well for the University if action is not swift.'

Thus it was that Peter Bullock, town constable, had been recruited to work with the University proctors to round up a group of scholars suspected of being the instigators of the riot at Oseney Abbey. Ten scholars were crammed in the tiny cell at the foot of the Great Keep in the west of Oxford. The cell was intended to house only one or two malefactors at a time, and even then the conditions were unpleasant. Purposely so, as no one once incarcerated relished returning. Now the situation was appalling. A tiny barred window was located high above the prisoners' heads, though from the outside it was barely noticeable at street level. Very little light penetrated even on the brightest days. Nor did it afford any breath of air from beyond the cell. Most of the young men stood shoulder to shoulder, barely able to move. The heat of their bodies made the cell unbearably hot, and the smell of sweat hung thickly in the air. One scholar sat on the urine-stained straw that covered the floor, his legs drawn up tight to his chest. Occasionally, someone moved to ease his tired limbs and one of those standing was pushed and stumbled against the hunched figure, cursing. He merely curled his arms tighter around his knees and stared blankly ahead.

Peter Bullock's own quarters were above the cell, at street level. It was sext, the day half gone, and William Falconer had appeared at his door. He wanted to interview the prisoners. Despite their friendship, Bullock was worried about Falconer's interference in such a sensitive matter. Not merely sensitive – the King himself was involved. But Falconer was persuasive.

'I simply wish to establish what happened. For my own satisfaction. I missed the crucial events and something is bothering me.'

Bullock knew to be worried when something bothered his friend. It meant that a straightforward criminal act would somehow become complicated and as convoluted as a snail shell. Falconer could sense his hesitancy.

'No one can blame you if, while you are out keeping the peace, a Master, well known for his uncontrollable curiosity, borrows your keys and talks to his students.'

The constable snorted.

'Borrows! Steals, more like.' But he knew he would have to give in and left Falconer with one plea.

'At least tell me what you learn. I don't even know if I've got the right students. Your lot aren't renowned for their honesty. And I am sure a few personal scores were being settled when I was given their names.'

He levered himself up on to his bowed legs and lurched out of the room, having dropped his bunch of keys on the pitted and stained table. He threw a comment over his shoulder.

'It's the big one you want.'

Falconer scooped up the heavy keys and walked through to the dingy yard overlooked on all sides by the Great Keep. A flight of stone steps led down to the great oaken door that incarcerated the students. At the bottom of the steps he selected the largest key on the battered ring and slid it into the lock. It turned easily, suggesting regular use. He pushed against the studded surface of the door and it swung into the cell. There was the sound of muffled curses as bodies shuffled back from the entrance.

Falconer detected fear in the exhalation of sweat that flowed from the cell. In the gloom even his poor vision could see that the eyes that fastened on to him were big with worry about what was to happen. He knew his large frame was intimidating, perhaps more so in the cell doorway now. As he didn't want, on this occasion at least, to frighten the students too much, he sat down on the bottom step of the flight that led to this little hell, and smiled gently.

'You all appear to be in some trouble.'

One of the students recognized him, and gasped in relief.

'Thank God, Master. Are you here to help us?'

'I may be able to, if you will help me.'

There was an unconscious surge of bodies towards him that stopped short of crossing the threshold, and Falconer knew they would do anything for him to gain their release. He also knew there was not much he could do to improve their situation now. However, he did not regret playing on their fears. They had been very foolish and deserved the incarceration they would suffer until someone negotiated a penance for their release. Falconer simply wanted the truth.

'Tell me what happened yesterday.'

Ann Segrim was a dutiful wife. It mattered little that her intelligence set her above her husband, Humphrey. She knew the lord of the manor of Botley grew angry if she displayed her greater knowledge, and would follow the ruling of the Dominican Friars and beat her. There was only one book he had read in his life, and that but briefly. It was a theological treatise written by Friar Nicolas Byard, and he relished quoting a particular passage as a threat. Ann could recite it by heart now, also.

'A man may chastise his wife and beat her for her correction, for she is of his household and therefore the lord may chastise his own.'

At the beginning of their marriage, arranged by her parents, she had feared her new husband, who was twenty years older than her. She had been selected for her good looks, and Humphrey had presumed she would be obedient. Unfortunately, Ann had assumed her new husband would welcome her contribution to the management of the estate. Did not her own father and mother share in the worries and the triumphs? She had been shocked and humiliated when her husband acted on Friar Byard's nostrum for the first time. It served only to make her angry and more wilful, which in its turn gave Segrim more reason to 'chastise'. But she had soon learned that her cleverness, not her wilfulness, would see her through. It became a pleasurable game to do exactly as she wished, without ever giving him cause for complaint. Soon she had tamed him, though he was unaware of it. And so she gave him no excuse to chastise her, though she did have to acquiesce to his amorous advances once in a while. Of late though these had considerably reduced, much to her private relief – perhaps because no children had been conceived in their ten years of marriage. Now her life was comfortable, if a little dull. Any distraction was a pleasure to her, and today was about to provide the beginnings of a significant distraction.

She heard voices in the courtyard that her chamber overlooked. One of them was her husband's, raised in anger, and she was curious to discover who he was berating. She gathered up the embroidery on which she was working, set it aside and crossed to the window. It was thickly glazed, and gave a green cast to the world beyond it. However, she could see Humphrey pacing up and down in the middle of the cobbled courtyard, waving his hands at a figure who stood under the arch of the gateway leading out to Segrim's considerable holdings. The other man was calm and motionless, in stark contrast to the agitated figure of her husband. Ann Segrim wished he would step forward so she could see who he was.

To stay one step ahead of her husband, she preferred to know exactly what business he was occupied with. Of late he had been more secretive than usual, and she had as yet been unable to fathom what he was involved in. It did require him to be away from the manor for many days at a time, so from that point of view she hoped it would continue. Her husband stopped his pacing and cast a look around him as though to ascertain no one was spying on his little conspiracy. She pressed back against the cold stone surrounding the window as he shot a glance up to her room. She waited a moment before daring to look out again, and almost missed the other man emerging from the shadow.

He was dressed in a cleric's robe, but unfortunately he had his hood pulled well over his head. Ann was unable to see his features, and then the figure turned and was gone. She sighed, returned to the comfortable chair beside the hearth, and picked up her embroidery again.

Falconer turned the key on the cell door and leaned back against it. He had learned some more about what had transpired yesterday. And what they had told him fitted well with what he had seen himself. It appeared that the group of students he had encountered on the road to Oseney Abbey had indeed gone to pay their respects to the Bishop, many in the hope of being granted favours in the form of lucrative benefices. No one could survive today without a favour from someone who wielded power. And Bishop Otho was powerful – doubly so. Appointed by the Pope, it was said he also had the ear of the King. Some in the group did not like the thought of appealing for help to a foreigner, but if needs must then anyone would swallow his pride.

Arriving at the gate soon after Falconer, they had encountered the Legate's bodyguard in the form of the thickset man the Regent Master had seen in the courtyard. They had been refused entrance by this man, but everyone had been relatively calm until another of the Bishop's retinue of servants entered the fray. He was passing through the courtyard with a pot full of hot water in his hands. Clearly feeling safe behind the squat frame of the bodyguard, he had apparently hurled abuse in his own tongue at the students. No one had understood what he said, but his supercilious Roman manner had been enough. A scuffle had broken out in the yard and the Roman servant had backed off.

Even then the matter might have been contained. But the servant, laden with his pot, had spotted the Irish chaplain whom Falconer had seen begging at the kitchen door. Without any provocation, the servant had thrown the scalding water all over the beggar. His scream alerted the students to what had happened, and a fellow feeling for the underdog roused their spirits. The incident immediately got out of hand and the bodyguard was beaten to the ground, overwhelmed by force of numbers.

At this point the story became confused. The students Falconer had questioned in the cell denied knowledge of an arrow being fired off. Certainly the servant had retreated behind the door leading to the guest hall and struggled to shut it in the students' faces. Some said they thought they had seen the Bishop in the doorway, but were not sure. They had after all seen him only briefly on his passage through Oxford. No one could say for sure if anyone else had appeared, until someone had spotted the Bishop, recognizable now by his episcopal robes, retreating from the rear of the hall through the cloisters. They had been unsuccessful in catching up with him before he had reached the sanctuary of the church. With the church door slammed in their face, they had had to be content with hurling abuse until the King's men had come to rescue the Bishop.

Of course, Falconer himself had witnessed these last scenes, and could understand why discretion had proved the better part of valour in the students' retreat. Unfortunately, they had spent the night in drunken boasting about their antics and there were enough people in Oxford willing to identify them the following morning. Now they were paying for their indiscretions. Falconer sighed, still needing more information about the events of yesterday.

He climbed the steps back up to the dank yard that more resembled a pit, surrounded as it was by the high walls of the Keep. The sun had already disappeared from his limited view and the yard was gloomy and cold. Shivering, he pulled his threadbare robe around him. At least he knew there was another student he could question. William Coksale had not been in the dungeon below, having obviously evaded the strong arms of Peter Bullock. He would no doubt be as difficult to dig out as a badger in his set, but Falconer would find him.

As the Regent Master strode off purposefully to seek his missing witness, he failed to notice a still, patient figure in the corner of the gloomy courtyard. The Templar was used to merging with the landscape, whether it be the sand-blown dunes of the Holy Land or the more mundane grey stones of a tower in Oxford. Falconer would have been surprised if he had known his interrogation of the students had been overheard. But Guillaume de Beaujeu had caught every word, admiring as he did the Regent Master's technique in eliciting the facts. He disdained the use of more forcible methods himself, by habit a persuader more than an extractor.

He had come to the jail under the Great Keep because he too wanted to speak with the students incarcerated there. After the events of yesterday, he needed to know the extent of the information they held in their heads. Could they impede the progress of his plans in England by revealing too much? Had his actions of yesterday been observed? The responses to most of Falconer's questions had in the main allayed his fears, and he was grateful to the man for asking them unwittingly on his behalf. But whatever the extent of his powers, he could not read minds and was thus unaware of Falconer's next intentions. He did know, however, that he could learn much by following this man, and he slipped from the shadows in pursuit.

The Third Seal

In the year 1247 a famine struck the nation. The unnatural floods of the previous year had swept away the crops and so what little corn there was cost as much as 20 solidos per quarter. Many therefore perished of hunger, and there was no succour in sight, for the abundant crops this year were once again flattened by autumnal rains. Thus was the Third Seal broken and there came forth a rider on a black horse. He held scales in his hands, wailing, 'A day's wage for a quart of flour.'

From the *Chronica Oseneiensis*

Chapter Five

Returning to Aristotle's Hall through the lanes that ran below the massive city walls, Falconer passed Little Gate. This cut through the wall's defences and gave the Dominicans access to the marshy and unhealthy island they inhabited outside the city. It also linked that land with the substantial property the order owned in St Ebbe's inside the city. Standing at the gate were two figures, merely a blur at this distance to Falconer's weak eyes. He went to pass the two, but closer he recognized one of the figures as a student of his, Hugh Pett. The boy was at the beginning of his studies, and his rich clothes betrayed him as someone from a wealthy family. His thin face, framed by carefully coifed red hair, was normally a picture of patrician composure. Now it was contorted with a horror reserved for the damned. The older man held him firmly by the arms and was shaking him.

'There is no hope, save for those Chosen by God. And they are few in number.'

The hectoring tones of the friar were familiar and, closer to, Falconer recognized him as the Dominican who had preached the imminence of the Apocalypse to the crowd in London. Now he was pouring out his vile warnings to one of Falconer's own students. The Dominican order, the so-called Preachers, had always irritated him. They set themselves up as superior in learning to the Franciscans, whom they called Minorites to belittle them. Heaven knows, but Falconer had little to thank the Franciscans for. Had they not virtually imprisoned his friend Roger Bacon? But at least they evinced a little humility. The Dominicans steadfastly refused to study the Arts, relying wholly on their theological background to dispute any subject. Since their arrival in Oxford, they had badgered the Jews of the town, and caused a few weak souls to convert to Christianity. Now they clearly wanted the whole populace on their knees in fear and trembling. He strode up to the pair.

'Master!' Hugh Pett's eyes were rounded in horror. Yet there was only a cold smile of satisfaction on the face of the friar as he turned towards Falconer.

'What have you been telling this boy?'

The youth spoke first in stammering tones.

'Master, Friar Fordam has come to tell us that the Last Judgement is near.'

Falconer snorted.

'Every few years, our preaching brethren predict the end of the world. And when it does not come, they claim the power of their prayers has saved us. It is a safe gamble.'

He fixed the friar with his penetrating blue eyes. 'And I would thank you not to hound one of my students.'

A dark expression clouded the truculent features of Friar Robert Fordam.

'Those who will not hear the truth are certainly not counted in the Chosen. And I did not force the truth upon this youth. It was he who followed me in his search for the right path.'

'It's true, Master,' blurted out the boy. 'I was told the friar was in Oxford and I wanted to hear his message.'

Falconer brushed Fordam aside and gently but firmly grasped Pett by the arm. He pulled him away from the friar.

'The only message you should pay attention to is what is taught you in the Schools. Learn and then make up your own mind.'

He put his arm around Pett's shoulder and went to walk him away. The friar stood framed in the arch of Little Gate, a blood red sun hanging over his left shoulder. He thundered a final warning to the susceptible youth.

'In Revelation, John warns us of a beast which rises from the earth. It resembles the Lamb, but speaks like a demon. It performs miracles and deludes the inhabitants of the earth. But it is brought down and chained by the Angels of Heaven. Look closely at those who lead you astray with seductive lies. Soon the evil Pope Alexander will die and then the Day of Judgement will be upon us.'

He slammed the gate shut behind him, and to Hugh Pett it could have been the gates of Heaven closing, with him on the wrong side.

Thomas de Cantilupe thought Humphrey Segrim was a very nervous man and he didn't know why. However, the man was, it seemed, intimate with people in the King's retinue. So the Chancellor-elect would do all he could to help him. Segrim had already intimated that de Cantilupe might be considered to join a select band of men who were working actively in the interests of the King. De Cantilupe was thus anxious to prove his worth.

'I can assure you that all the students known to have been involved in yesterday's outrage are now incarcerated in the Great Keep. I await instruction from the King as to what should be done with them.'

Segrim paced up and down the stone floor of de Cantilupe's temporary residence, the fresh rushes crackling under his feet. His anxiety transmitted itself to the other man, who shifted uncomfortably in his chair. Or perhaps it was the hair shirt that de Cantilupe habitually wore that caused his present discomfort. He wore it to remind him of the pains of the world, and to punish him for taking pleasures where others could not – pleasures like good food and wine, to which he was particularly susceptible. The Chancellor-elect had a thin face with a hooked Roman nose and flushed cheeks. He kept the expression on it now as solemn as possible, though he ached for the excellent meal his cook had prepared him, which was rapidly spoiling. He had been at the table surveying the steaming meat-balls when old Halegod anxiously announced the unexpected arrival of Humphrey Segrim.

De Cantilupe sadly cast his eye on the fancifully decorated balls covered in yellow and green batter, served up with onions and beans, and pushed himself back from the table. Now he recalled the meal and wondered if it could be saved. He spurred the other man on.

'Perhaps you know of the King's wishes in this matter?'

Segrim stopped his pacing and stood over the Chancellor-elect, large and menacing. A sly smile forced itself to his lips.

'Not at this moment. But I can enquire – the King is in Abingdon with the Lord Bishop still. I shall send a messenger to discover His Majesty's wishes. In the meantime, I think I'll have a word with the constable. What's his name?'

De Cantilupe knew that Segrim was well aware of the name but feigned ignorance of such menials. He furnished Peter Bullock's name, and Segrim wrapped his fur-trimmed robe around his large frame and left. The Chancellor-elect hurried to his kitchens, in the fading hope that the food would still tempt his discerning palate.

Falconer led a life a little more frugal than either de Cantilupe or Humphrey Segrim. He earned twelve pence a year for each of his series of lectures, and there was an income to be made from the students lodging in Aristotle's Hall. But his rents left him with little to satisfy even his simple pleasures. However, he did not care greatly for the mundane and physical, when other stimulating matters were available to tempt his mind. He had sent Hugh Pett out to risk the unruly atmosphere of Oxford in the evening to see if he could uncover the whereabouts of the missing student, William Coksale. While he waited, he occupied his mind with sifting through Friar Bacon's papers.

Once again the paper on the waking trance seemed to draw his fingers to it, and he reread the crabbed text, painstakingly written by his absent friend in circumstances Falconer could not imagine. It seemed that, by using a magical intonation and making certain passes with the fingers, a susceptible person could be induced to carry out acts they were incapable of in a waking state. Although the victim was in a trance, he seemed to be alert and normal in every way, until a magic word was spoken or a certain circumstance occurred. Then the victim carried out the wishes of the trance-maker.

Something hovered around the back of Falconer's skull, buzzing like a fly on raw meat. It was about to disappear when Hugh Pett thrust his head around the door of Falconer's chamber. Before the youth could speak, Falconer remembered.

'The friar from London!'

The young man looked puzzled and hesitated to disturb his master.

'Hugh, don't hang around the door. You've just reminded me of something that was threatening to drive me mad if it had not come to me.'

Pett still did not know to what his master referred. But he was used to his strange moods.

'Anyway, tell me if your errand has been successful. Have you found Coksale?'

'I cannot be sure, but . . .'

Hugh hesitated, and Falconer urged him on.

'Come, don't be shy. Tell me what you have discovered.'

'Well, I have not checked this for myself, but I have searched everywhere he might otherwise be with no success.'

He grinned broadly, and Falconer noticed for the first time that he looked a little dishevelled.

'I will not tell you the number of taverns I have been in tonight.'

'I thought you looked somewhat flushed. I will discipline you later for that transgression. In the meantime . . .?'

'I had almost given up, but decided to go back to his lodgings. One of his friends at Hart Hall says he always turns to St Frideswide when in trouble. So, if he's not in hiding in some friend's clothes chest, or burying his head in some ale jug, I can only suggest—'

Falconer interrupted.

'That he is in the church not a hundred yards from where we are now. Thank you, Hugh.'

Pett smiled shyly and retreated from the room, before Falconer could remember about his drinking escapade.

Although it was dark outside, and Oxford was not an entirely safe place at night, Falconer resolved to find Coksale immediately. Anyway, the Regent Master had not always been a man purely of the mind and could defend himself. He was used to nocturnal ramblings, and had not yet been assaulted by a nightwalker. He guessed that Coksale on the other hand would now be cold, hungry and extremely afraid – an admirable combination to make the youth succumb to Falconer's questioning. A quick trip to the kitchen to retrieve some leftovers from supper, and he would be ready.

He had already gathered a number of truths, and needed some time to compare one with another until the greater truth, deduced and not given, emerged. His immersion in Aristotelian logic had furnished him with a method for solving crimes, and his fondness for discovering the truth gave him the cause to make use of it. He wondered if his chance discovery of the waking trance in Bacon's papers also provided a truth. Already he thought he saw how Friar Fordam entranced his audience. However, that seemed to have nothing to do with the death of the Bishop's master of cooks. Or not directly at least. He did wonder about one of the students he had seen apparently entranced. He, and therefore the friar, could be closely involved with the murder. But he needed more information first, and perhaps Coksale could help him with that.

The to and fro of messengers had piqued Ann Segrim's curiosity. As she heard her husband retiring to his room, which was the only other private chamber in this spartan house, she arranged to appear at her door as if meeting him by accident on the upper landing. He stopped abruptly before her, resembling a rearing horse startled by a snake. She hoped he thought of her as a harmless grass-snake.

'I did not see you at supper.'

'I had business to transact with de Cantilupe, who is to be the new Chancellor of the University.'

Segrim was his usual curt self, especially when it came to business. He did not consider it fitting for a woman to be involved in men's affairs. Ann realized that to achieve her aim would not be easy, and linked her arm with her husband's, drawing him into her private chamber. A look of curiosity on his face was soon replaced with a sly, lascivious sneer. She hoped she could discover what she wanted before she gave him occasion to think she was offering to share his bed. Seating him comfortably in the chair close to the fire, she called her maid and enquired of her husband if he wished something to drink. Segrim had a good cellar of wine from Poitou, and the maid was despatched on an errand to fetch some.

Ann began her interrogation as a dutiful wife enquiring about the running of the estate. Not that she wanted or expected to be given too much information. To enquire showed obedience, to expect a sensible reply betokened shrewishness. Anyway, Ann Segrim discovered all she needed to know about the running of Humphrey's estate from his clerk. She smiled sweetly as her husband plied her with assurances of the smooth running of all his affairs. This she knew was contrary to the truth. Under gentle pressure from her, his clerk had recently expressed a fear that much of the income of the estate was disappearing elsewhere – so much so that it could be ruinous in a year or two. Ann needed to know what was happening to the money before he, and therefore she, became a pauper.

As her maid poured Segrim a cup of wine, in goodly measure thanks to the unspoken glance from Ann to the servant, she asked in her usual ingenuous tone about the recent activity in the courtyard. The childish timbre of her voice irritated her, but served to put Humphrey off his guard. He could not conceive of his wife as being devious, or having the wit to unravel the affairs of men. Besides, given the chance, he was inclined to boast to her of his connections. A foolish grin spread over his face, and he took a deep draught of Poitou to keep up the suspense. Finally, he could not restrain his pleasure.

'I have been in touch with His Majesty the King at Abingdon.'

Ann's eyes rounded in genuine surprise. Her husband had never been so ambitious before. Seeing that she was impressed, he was moved to continue.

'I am involved with a group of very important people, who are intimately concerned with ensuring the wishes of the King are carried out. Naturally I cannot give you their names, but suffice it to say that they are all men of the King's court.'

In self-important tones, he did make clear that this party required funds, which he was well able to supply, and that preferment was assured. Ann knew the former was not true, and was certain the latter could not be relied on. But Humphrey pressed ahead.

'Of course, His Majesty is a little unworldly and sometimes we have to make decisions that he must be protected from. These unruly students, for instance. We have decided that something drastic needs to be done, if the Bishop is to be mollified.'

At this point he slumped back in his chair and smiled secretively into his empty wine cup. Ann sighed, and began to assess whether she needed to know more. And whether finding out was worth suffering the drunken gropings of her husband.

The church of St Frideswide was icy cold, and the spring evening had descended into darkness. The massive stone pillars supporting the great rounded arches of the nave cast heavy shadows swallowing the fitful light of tallow candles on the altar. Falconer sat in the body of the nave apparently oblivious to these discomforts.

He was humming a tune he had recently heard his students singing, the words of which seemed to fit the circumstances of yesterday. He softly sang the first few lines:

'Roma caput mundi est
Sed nihil capit mundum . . .'

As he mouthed the words, he unwrapped the cloth he had on his lap to reveal a hunk of bread and some ripe cheese. He broke off a corner of the bread and chewed contentedly on it, still humming the irreverent song. He showed no surprise when a figure slipped out of the gloom of the north transept and sat hesitantly at the opposite end of the bench.

'William. You must be famished.'

He pushed the cloth bundle of food along the length of the wooden bench. For a moment, William Coksale just looked, then hungrily grabbed the bread. As he ate, Falconer began to talk gently to the fugitive student.

'The crypt must be a chilly place, even in the spring.'

Coksale nodded ruefully, his mouth full of cheese.

'And the sole company of the revered saint's body may be a comfort, but hardly conducive to good conversation. Tell me what happened, and I promise I will help you.'

Once Coksale had broken his silence, his story came brimming over, like the froth from a poorly tapped beer barrel. He was anxious to tell what had occurred and Falconer was as anxious to hear.

The youth confirmed the events leading up to the pitched battle as he had seen them. The banter with the Bishop's bodyguard had been reasonable, until a janitor with a bowl of something hot had got excited about the students. He had thrown the contents of his bowl over a beggar, who he must have thought was one of the students. So far the story tallied with what Falconer had heard from the other students. But at this point Coksale hesitated.

Falconer suddenly understood why he was in such fear for his life.

'You saw who fired the arrow.'

Coksale nodded and looked at the ground, his fingers kneading the last scrap of bread to a grey ball.

'You must tell me.'

Coksale looked Falconer in the eye, and explained. Several of the students carried weapons – that was nothing unusual in itself – and more than one had a bow and some arrows slung over his back.

'But no one thought to use them, until the Bishop appeared at the door.'

'The Bishop? I was told he was entertaining guests.' Falconer had dismissed the others' suggestions that they might have seen the Bishop at the main door. It simply did not fit. But here was Coksale telling him the same story.

'How did you know it was the Bishop?'

'Because several of us had seen him arrive in Oxford earlier in the day. He had ridden down the High Street in full view of everyone.'

Falconer restrained his disbelief and motioned for Coksale to continue.

'When the janitor threw the water over the beggar, the Bishop laughed and that was when I saw him. John Gryffin, the Welshman.'

Coksale said the Welshman seemed agitated by the Bishop's reaction, and pulled his bow from over his shoulder. He notched an arrow and let it fly just as the Bishop turned to go back in the guest hall. No one had seen it hit, and when the Bishop was spotted leaving the rear of the hall, Coksale had assumed the arrow had missed. It was only later the students had heard that someone had been killed.

'It was an accident. It was the Bishop who was the target.'

'You're sure you saw Bishop Otho at the door?'

The youth was a picture of earnest honesty.

'Yes. Of course he didn't have his papal robe on. But several of those who were with me saw him too, and named him.' Coksale grinned ruefully. 'Not very politely, as a simonist and a usurer.'

Falconer smiled encouragingly, so Coksale asked him what to do.

'I would go back to your lodgings now.'

'But what about the hue and cry?' Coksale glanced nervously at the doorway of the church as if afraid to leave its sanctuary.

'I think you'll find they've taken all the culprits they wish to take. Just keep your head down over the next few days. And don't go upsetting any more Papal Legates.'

Coksale stumbled his thanks and hastily left the church. Falconer listened to the echoes of his feet on the stone floor as he pondered what he had now learned. It could not have been the Bishop at the door, yet Coksale and the others said it was. If the man they saw was the master of cooks, then his turning his back on the melee in the courtyard could account for the arrow in his back. But there were other facts Falconer could not fit in with this theory. There were more truths to be collected yet. And now he knew it was a Welshman who fired the arrow, he was anxious to talk to the incarcerated students again. He could not recall speaking with one who had a Welsh accent, but he did remember someone who had remained seated in the corner of the cell throughout his interrogations. Perhaps this was the elusive bowman.

The hour was now too late to return to the Great Keep. Peter Bullock would not thank him for being roused at such a time. He would have to return in the morning after his lectures had been dutifully delivered. He rose and stole out of the church, soon to be lost in the dank, swirling mist that filled the lane.

After a few minutes, Guillaume de Beaujeu stepped from behind the heavy stone pillar that helped support the nave and gently eased his frozen muscles back to life.

Chapter Six

Regent Master Falconer's lectures were always well attended. The early morning was set aside for so-called ordinary lectures, given by Masters. These required the students to listen like children being taught the Catechism. Cursory lectures, given by Masters and more junior members of the University, took place in the afternoon, and were much less formal and more disputatious. Whatever the hour, Master Falconer's lectures were anything but ordinary, by any meaning of the expression. Seduced by the philosophy of Aristotle, Falconer gave lectures on logic which revolved around the latest theories being discovered as the Greek's original texts were translated into Latin. For the students the extra pleasure was that the Church did not fully approve of Aristotle.

This morning was no different from any other at one of the Master's lectures. The sun had barely crawled over the ramparts of the city, but his lecture room in the little back street behind the crumbling façade of St Mary's Church was crowded. Falconer was already in full flow. He spurned the raised dais on which the Regent Master was expected to sit, robed in fur-trimmed splendour and wearing the tufted biretta on his head. He preferred to squat on the narrow benches with his students, or pace up and down the aisles between, shooting questions at all and sundry. He was on his favourite topic.

'The study of the natural sciences, zoology, botany, and alchemy, shows us that only by exact observation can we come to the attainment of truth. In the words of Abelard, a doctrine should not be believed simply because God has said it, but because we are convinced by reason it is so.'

There was a buzz of excitement at this apparently heretical statement. Falconer smiled and softened it a little.

'Of course if you wish to dispute this, go to doubting Thomas. I refer, of course, to Thomas Aquinas whose view is that philosophy – examining the natural order – and theology – examining the supernatural – are two different truths. And therefore need not contradict each other. Convenient, perhaps. Especially for such a conformist as Thomas. Now that is all you are getting today.'

There was a general groan of disappointment from the students. As some began to voice their protest, Falconer shouted them down.

'I have some exact observations to make of my own. So go away and think for yourselves.'

As Hugh Pett shuffled past him in the queue of students leaving the room, Falconer tapped him on the shoulder and thrust the key to the room into his hand.

'Lock up for me, Hugh. I'm in a hurry.'

Hugh nodded his acquiescence, and Falconer pressed through the crowd of students, who stood back respectfully for the Master. Outside the Schools, he crossed the street and hurried west down the narrow lane opposite. His burly figure almost filled the space between the crudely built houses, which over his head seemed to lean across the lane and depend on their neighbour opposite for support. There were a few, poorer students' halls here – Hawk's and White's – but the area needed pulling down. Falconer wondered why people didn't build more in stone as they did in the Jewish quarter, although it was said the Jews built in stone only to prevent their houses being burned to the ground in times of trouble. Falconer didn't blame them, if that was the case. He crossed Northgate Street, the debris of yesterday's market still swirling in the light morning breeze, and plunged down another alley opposite.

Finally, he emerged close under the high walls of the Great Keep. He hoped that Peter Bullock was up and about. He could be like a bear with a sore head when disturbed. But Falconer was impatient to interrogate the Welshman in Bullock's custody, and would brave a raging bear to satisfy his curiosity. Fortunately, he spotted the constable in the dingy courtyard as he approached. At least the man was not in bed and needing to be woken. But as he was about to hail his friend, Falconer noticed that the heavy oaken door to the cell was open wide. And no students were visible.

'What's happened? Where are your prisoners?'

'You're too late.' Bullock's leathery face wore a grim smile. 'They've been taken to Wallingford. And no doubt thence to London.'

'When did this happen?'

Bullock took Falconer's arm and led him inside. Once seated in Bullock's sparsely furnished room, and taking up the offer of a fresh flagon of ale, Falconer was told the events of the early hours of the morning. Bullock had been disturbed soon after midnight, as far as he could estimate it, by an insistent knocking on his street door. Cautiously opening it with his trusty club in his hand, he had been confronted with a small troop of soldiers. A haughty man, who claimed himself to be the Earl de Warenne, and who had been the one trying to knock his door down, abruptly demanded the students be handed over to his custody. Over Bullock's protests, he had produced a document with the seal of the King on the bottom. Reluctantly, Bullock had roused the sleepy students and they had been unceremoniously loaded on to a cart drawn up beneath the tower.

'The last I saw of them, they were disappearing in the direction of South Gate.'

Falconer cursed and unrolled the King's scroll that Bullock had offered as proof of his story. The seal did indeed bear the King's arms, but many people in his service could have used it. But then, why should he doubt that this was a simple move by the King to punish the University? Why should he suspect some underhand means of preventing him finding the truth? He laughed wryly at his foolish sense of self-importance. No, this was ill-timed for him, but still a straightforward movement of prisoners. Or so he thought, until Bullock added some disturbing information.

'Of course, it was only then that I saw riding with the soldiers there was a civilian. And he seemed to be more in charge than the so-called Earl. Unfortunately he was too well wrapped in his cloak for me to see him clearly.'

It was Brother Peter Talam's duty that morning to work in St John's Hospital. This was a long, low-roofed building with a prominent tower situated outside East Gate. The main part of the hospital was quite new, dwarfing the crude little structure that had been simply a place for the poor and needy to die. It had started with Ralph Harbottle's predecessor as abbot. He had discovered a treasure-house of medical books at Oseney, and had encouraged the study of medicine by his brethren. Soon, leeching the monks had become a regular practice to encourage a healthy regime at the abbey. On becoming abbot, Ralph himself had wished to continue the regime, but was desirous of benefiting the greater community as well as the monastic one. First he enlarged the hospital, and then employed an elderly medicus with compendious knowledge of herbal cures to work at St John's. Now the hospital was rededicated to people requiring 'to recover their health and necessity'. The care of lepers was largely left to St Bartholomew's, which boasted a saintly relic – a piece of Saint Bartholomew's skin – as remedy. Strictly speaking, monastic vows and the fiat of Pope Alexander III forbade the practice of medicine by monks outside the abbey. But most brothers were expected to render assistance at the hospital. Today Talam had ensured it was his turn, as he had a reason of his own to visit the hospital. Hurrying down the High Street, he pondered on his next move with the Papal Legate. His plans to prevaricate over the exact sums due from the abbey had paid off unexpectedly due to the murder. Should he expect the man to return and demand his dues? Or could he now expect him to have been permanently scared off? Whatever course of action Bishop Otho took, he must prepare himself for the worst.

Once through East Gate, Talam had only a short distance to go. The hospital was sited a safe and sanitary distance from the gates of the city. Its only near neighbour was the Jewish cemetery, and no one there was going to worry about the diseased inmates of St John's. Entering through the main door, Talam hurried through the lofty hall, divided into small wooden cubicles behind whose doors the moans of the infirm and dying were contained. He rushed past the stench of the latrine block and knelt at the altar of the end chapel, offering up a mumbled prayer. To the left of the chapel was the small structure that had been the old hospital before its considerable enlargement. He had argued with Ralph Harbottle about the expense of such a project. But the Abbot was amassing his store of good works for the day he entered heaven, and insisted on the new building.

Peter Talam closed the door behind him, and breathed a sigh of relief. He could not bear the interminable noises the suffering made, and preferred to carry out his duties in this small room. Along one wall were serried ranks of jars and boxes that held the herbs and other remedies used by the medicus of the hospital. Talam was a little suspicious of the treatments used by the old man in some cases. The medicus seemed still to believe in fairies, and such symptoms as livid fingernails and watery eyes he persisted in diagnosing as something he was fond of calling water-elf. The remedy involved incantations. However, the old man did resort to many herbal cures whose efficacy Talam was witness to, and he had learned valuable skills over the years. He had also learned to handle the herbs with care, as many of them had powerful effects – some more deadly than curative. He read along the shelves – henbane, calvewort, horehound, verbena, clover, celandine, mandrake, woodruff, dill, gorse. He could not find what he sought and poked amongst the boxes on a lower shelf. The well-worn labels proclaimed more ancient remedies – badger's teeth, hare's gall, wolf hair. These were no good to him, and he returned to the shelves of herbs. There he found it, hidden behind jars of yarrow and rue. The label read 'foxglove'. He just managed to hide the jar in his purse before the elderly medicus shuffled into the room to prepare his potions. Talam pottered around for a while, then made his excuses and left. He had much to do that day.

Peter Bullock wished he had not been persuaded by Master Falconer to accompany him to Wallingford. The journey was barely ten miles, but Bullock was no horseman. They had not long left East Gate, turning south to skirt Cowley Marsh, and his arse was already sore. And the dry weather had soon turned the muddy tracks into dusty cratered obstacle courses. He was glad at least that Falconer had selected a docile nag for him. If the Master kept his interrogations short, they would be back to Oxford before dark. Surely the matter would not take long – it was madness to contemplate travelling the countryside after the sun had set.

He hacked along a few yards behind Falconer, who seemed much more at home on horseback. Bullock was not surprised by any of the man's accomplishments. Since they had met over a row between a snotty student and a penny-pinching baker, Bullock had learned little about the past of the man. But he did know that Falconer's practical knowledge seemed endless, and that he could turn his hand skilfully to things other Masters of the University disdained.

His wandering thoughts were brought back to earth as he almost rode his nag into the rear of Falconer's horse. They had reached the village of Nuneham, and Bullock assumed Falconer was uncertain of his way.

'The route to Wallingford is straight on.'

Falconer smiled.

'I know. But while we are so near Abingdon, I think I will crave an audience with My Lord Bishop.'

Bullock groaned, and saw their chances of returning to Oxford the same day receding into the mists. Falconer spurred his horse into action and turned down the track that led to Abingdon. Bullock was mystified how the Regent Master was going to gain access to the Bishop, but was quite prepared to assume he could.

In fact it turned out to be simple. Once they had entered the main courtyard of the old abbey where the King kept his royal chambers, Falconer whispered in the ear of the surly steward who approached the dusty travellers. The man commanded them to stay where they were, but soon returned with a different look on his face. He obsequiously beckoned Falconer up the steps to the main entrance door, thrusting his horse's reins at Bullock. He clearly took the older man for Falconer's servant, and expected him to wait outside. Falconer shrugged an apology to Bullock and followed the steward. Bullock decided he might as well benefit from his temporary demotion and went in search of the kitchens.

Falconer, meanwhile, was led down a long corridor opulently hung with richly coloured tapestries. His footsteps echoed on the tiled floor, and he half expected the King himself to emerge from one of the many doors that opened on to the corridor. He began to wonder if he were out of his depth here. Suddenly he was being ushered through a door at the end of the corridor, and found himself confronted by a thin, scruffily dressed man with the face of a trader who has just found a counterfeit coin in his takings. This could not be the Papal Legate. Perhaps he was not going to be allowed to see the Bishop after all.

Just as the acid-faced man started a whining interrogation of Falconer's credentials, a large figure emerged from the inner door of the chamber and cut him off.

'Please, Boniface, I do not have time for all this.'

The large man clasped Falconer's arm and led him into the inner room. There he drew him over to two seats arranged in the window. Falconer looked round but the secretary had already discreetly withdrawn.

'You say you are an emissary from the Chancellor of the University with news of the killing.'

The Bishop had a distinctly Roman accent, but a good command of the language. To Falconer he appeared genuinely anxious to hear some news. This proved awkward, as he had none to give. His feigned position was created on the spur of the moment to gain him entry. As he attempted to say much and at the same time very little to the Bishop, he studied the man. His florid face and bulbous nose reminded him of someone he had seen recently. It was only when he came to the end of his fairytale of a report that he was stunned into realizing he had last seen the Bishop's features face down in a sea of blood and spoilt food. Otho bore an uncanny resemblance to the dead master of cooks.

'You bring me some comfort that my brother's death will be avenged. Of course I would not expect less of your King.'

Falconer realized that the Bishop had confirmed the resemblance to the dead man. He now understood why the Bishop had appeared to be at both the front and rear entrances of the guest hall at Oseney Abbey in different garb at almost the same moment.

'Forgive me, Your Grace. I did not know the master of cooks had been your brother. I naturally assumed that being in such a position he was . . .'

The Bishop supplied the words.

'Of lower rank? But you see in my position I needed someone I could trust to taste my food. Especially recently. And who better than my own brother?'

He explained to Falconer that since his arrival in England several attempts had been made on his life. Now the only person he trusted totally had been killed.

'Of course there are those who told me my brother was not to be trusted either. I have even had the cautionary tale of Cain and Abel thrust at me as an example. *"And he was jealous of God's pleasure with his brother's offering."* Oh yes. But I have known Sinibaldo since his birth. How long have they known him?'

The Bishop rose from his seat and Falconer realized his brief audience was at an end. As they walked towards the door, Falconer asked which of his guests had absented themselves during their audience with him at Oseney. Otho was puzzled by the question, but named all the supplicants and affirmed that no one had left before the affray. Suddenly there was a clamour from the other room and the Bishop's secretary burst in, ashen-faced. Otho crossed to Boniface and leaned over as the little man whispered urgently into his ear. A strange look crossed the heavy features of the Bishop, and he turned to Falconer with an apology.

'I am sorry – you must leave now. I have had some . . . terrible news. We have just now been informed that His Holiness Pope Alexander is dead. I must go and pray for his soul.'

As Falconer was ushered back down the seemingly endless corridor, he could not help but ponder on the look on the Bishop's face as he had learned of the death of the Pope. Not horror, or sadness, merely naked ambition.

Leaving the messenger to carry his doleful news to the rest of the kingdom, Richard de Sotell, the Dominican Friar-Senior, offered up a short prayer and breathed a sigh of relief when he heard of the death of Pope Alexander. Looking out of his austere cell over the island between Trill Mill stream and the Thames, he pondered on the early days when his order arrived in Oxford. They had settled in the heart of Jewry and eagerly sought converts. They had cheerfully made enemies of the lazy monks at Oseney Abbey, and spread their preaching across the country-side. It had all seemed so simple.

Then the Franciscans had arrived, and challenged their position of pious superiority. As a young friar he recalled generously housing and feeding the first Franciscans to enter Oxford. They had shared a fellowship in God – until the Minorites tried to outdo his order in humility and poverty.

'Bare feet and mean garments, indeed,' murmured the ancient friar to no one but the birds who fluttered below his window picking up the spilt grain from the mill. He far preferred the company of the beasts of the field and the birds of the air. He leaned against the rough stone of the window frame and rubbed his chest as the stabbing pain clutched at him again. In a few moments it was gone and he breathed easier, pondering what the Pope's death meant for his order.

The two orders' battle for the moral ascendancy had led to a condemnation of the power and wealth of the Pope and all his representatives. The old man found this an uncomfortable doctrine to live with. Not so his younger brethren, who happily espoused a dislike of anything related to the indulgence of the Papacy. Perhaps the death of Alexander would keep hot-heads like Robert Fordam quiet for a while – at least until they had another focus for their hate elected. He must tell the young man the news as soon as he could find him.

The trip from Abingdon to Wallingford had been completed with hardly a word passing between the two men. Falconer had briefly told Bullock the news about the Pope, then had lapsed into silence. Bullock recognized the man's habitual method of sorting the truths he had collected and kept quiet also. In fact he was regretting the ample repast he had managed to scrounge from the Bishop's servants. Each lurch of his horse threatened to deprive him of the meal. He was glad when the walls of Wallingford Castle came into view, especially as the day was well advanced. But an extended interview might still necessitate staying in the town overnight.

The castle's dark-stained walls were a depressing sight to the Regent Master. The whole squat and lugubrious pile seemed to be sinking under its own weight into the ground on which it stood. It must have been an awful prospect to the students doomed to be incarcerated in it. Falconer was glad he had brought Peter Bullock with him. The constable's presence gave him some legal standing when he asked of the warden of Wallingford Castle to see the students who had been transferred from Oxford.

At first the old warrior was reluctant to allow anyone to see his charges. But Peter Bullock took him to one side and carried on a murmured conversation that Falconer could not catch. Unlike at Abingdon, here it was the constable who gained entry. But this time both men were given access to those they wished to see.

As they were led down a dank, gloomy passage, the old man kept glancing at the Regent Master with a look of contempt on his face. As he fumbled with his keys at an ancient barred door, Falconer pulled Bullock to one side and asked him quietly how he had persuaded the reluctant warden to admit them.

'No doubt the same way you did at Abingdon.'

'I lied.'

'And so did I.' He laughed. 'I told him you were enamoured of the Welshman and had threatened to kill yourself if you could not see him again.'

Falconer hooted with laughter, and the old man looked over his shoulder with a gaze of pity for this madman. Bullock went on.

'Of course he would have let you finish yourself off there and then. And offered you his sword to do it with. What really persuaded him was the coin I slipped in his palm.'

The warden's trembling hands at last negotiated the unlocking of the door that led to the dungeons. On the other side, two or three tallow lamps burned fitfully, constantly threatening to die in the icy wind that blew through the open door. Water cascaded off the walls at weak points in the stonework. The river was nearby, and they were now below its level. Falconer heard weary voices behind the nearest door, crying out for food. He felt sorry for the young men, who were learning a harsh lesson about power and authority.

'The Welshman?' croaked the old man, asking for confirmation.

'Yes, John Gryffin, the Welshman,' said Bullock, used to the terse nature of those who worked in the same drab business as himself. The warden crooked an already talon-like finger and led them on.

'He's on his own. Lucky boy has the best accommodation we can offer.'

Falconer realized the old man considered this a joke when a rictus of a grin crossed his lined face, and a strange wheezing noise escaped his toothless mouth. He was still laughing when he swung open the door of the Welshman's cell.

John Gryffin was in no fit state to appreciate the joke. At first neither Falconer nor Bullock spotted him. They were looking on the slimy floor of the cell, spread with a thin layer of mouldy straw. It was only when they looked up in puzzlement they saw the shape hanging from a beam that ran the width of the tiny cell. John Gryffin's face was an inhuman mask. His eyes were popping out of his head, his features a livid red as though he were straining mightily to lift an impossible load. His mouth was thrown open in a silent cry for help. A cord that formerly must have held his tunic tight at his waist was stretched between his neck and the beam. It creaked as the body swayed in the breeze caused by the opening of the cell door.

For a few moments everyone stood still, like a tableau in a miracle play. Then Bullock leapt forward, his knife in his hand to cut the youth down. Gently he cradled him in his arms and brought John Gryffin back to earth, but he knew he was already dead. The corpse was cold.

The Fourth Seal

In the year 1248 strange fires throughout the lands of Europe reduced many towns to ashes. The cathedral of Saint Peter in Cologne was destroyed, as were countless towns in France and Normandy. In England, much of Newcastle was destroyed by fire, without cause from heat or drought. Monstrous births were reported. On the Isola Vectis a mannikin of perfect proportions was seen who, in his eighteenth year, was only three feet tall. In the Welsh borders a giant was born who at six months had all his teeth and was as large as a seventeen year old. Thus was the Fourth Seal broken, which Revelation tells us caused the appearance of another horse, sickly pale. On its back was Death with the power to kill with pestilence and wild beasts.

From the *Chronica Oseneiensis*

Chapter Seven

'What's all the fuss about? The fool killed himself, didn't he?' The old warden's lip trembled at the thought he might lose a lucrative living over this death. 'It will save the King money, keeping him locked up.'

His two visitors still knelt beside the cold body of John Gryffin. The obvious conclusion was that the boy had killed himself out of a sense of shame and guilt. But the ever suspicious Falconer had carefully scrutinized the body, and particularly the ligature around its neck. Delicately pulling the coarse cord from around the unfortunate student's throat, he peered closely at the livid mark he found underneath. Taking Bullock's arm, he pulled him down and pointed. It was clear that there was a much thinner red line around the circumference of his whole neck, marked at regular intervals with circular discoloration. Falconer rose to his feet.

'It is obvious that this cord was not the cause of his death.' He fingered the lengthy waist band, which had clearly been wound twice around the waist. 'He was strangled with something much finer.'

The warden blanched at the thought of someone in his custody being murdered – and not by the proper authorities. Falconer continued.

'Anyway, look around you. There is not so much as a stool in this cell.' He cut off the warden's protests with a sweep of his hand. As though the fool need excuse the foul conditions in which he held his prisoners. Anyway, this one no longer cared. He stared at the body on the slimy, cold ground.

'My point is, the beam is too high for him to have reached up, attached the rope, then put the noose around his neck.'

'He could have thrown the rope over,' the old man responded feebly.

'What, and then pulled himself up by the neck and held on until he had strangled himself?' Falconer's response was scornful. The important issue now was to discover the murderer.

Falconer had thought to begin by gently coaxing the frightened man into providing the necessary information. But Bullock was impatient, and thrust the startled Falconer aside. Grasping the old man's greasy jerkin with his calloused hands, he shoved him against the clammy wall, with a force that Falconer feared would snap his brittle bones.

'You must tell me who has been in these cells since the Oxford students arrived.'

Despite his crooked back, Peter Bullock's upper body was powerful, and he used it to the fullest effect to intimidate the old warden. His previous comradely treatment of the man was now entirely absent. The old fool did not deserve to be considered an equal. Bullock now stood towering over him, holding his fist in the man's terrified face. Spittle dribbled out of the warden's toothless mouth as he reviewed the failures of his custodial duties.

'There was some noble lord who came soon after they arrived. Said he was on the King's business. It was he who told me to put the Welshman into a separate cell. Said he was dangerous.'

'And his name?'

'I don't know.'

Bullock twisted the man's jerkin tight until he began to choke. With a cough, he spat out the name.

'Segrim.'

'And who else?'

The warden fought to control a coughing fit, and nervously wrapped his bony fingers around his neck. He decided there was no point in hiding the truth – he had already been well paid for turning a blind eye.

'This morning, some priest came. Wanted to console the students, he said. Who am I to keep someone from their communion with God?'

'A priest? What sort?'

'What do you mean, what sort?' The old man was getting nervous again – this time the crooked-back man would surely kill him. But he really didn't know what he wanted.

'A monk, a friar, a bishop?'

The warden laughed edgily.

'Not a bishop! It must have been a friar.'

Falconer's eyes glinted.

'Or a monk. What's the difference?'

While Falconer and Bullock were carrying out their exasperating interrogation of the warden, Guillaume de Beaujeu was spurring his way back to Oxford. His time in Wallingford had been well spent, and he now understood who were his enemies in the battle for the Papacy. It might be that the heart of the conflict lay hundreds of miles away in Rome, but the long arms of conspiracy spread all over Christendom. And nowhere more so than in England, here and now. His instructions from the Grand Master had been specific, but Guillaume was always his own man. He carried out his own assessment of the benefits to his order of one side or the other in such a crucial struggle, and saw no conflict with his vow of obedience. His obedience was to the Order of the Knights of the Temple of Solomon, and the Grand Master was only one individual in a long line. Besides, he had desires to be Grand Master himself soon.

He cursed the two days' delay he had incurred in London, due to the inattention of the master of the Temple commanderie. If he had arrived sooner things might have gone differently at Oseney Abbey. Nevertheless he did not regret now having to fall back on his own resources. He preferred to perform a solitary role in all his undertakings. That way, he had no one to blame but himself if things went awry. Not that they ever did – he was a careful, calculating man. When luck came his way, he used it, but did not rely on it. He had been lucky to find the warden of Wallingford Castle fast asleep at his post, no doubt tired out by a busy and disrupted night incarcerating the Oxford students. How easy it had been to borrow his keys. And his luck had held, when he found the Welshman in a cell all on his own.

Guillaume de Beaujeu rode into Oxford through South Gate just as darkness fell. Regent Master Falconer and his companion were not so lucky and had to stay in a squalid inn at Wallingford for the night. This gave Falconer much time to brood over his investigations, but he was unable to find the greater truth of who murdered both the Welshman and the Papal Legate's master of cooks. The tapestry of events had too many loose ends hanging for him to be able to see the full picture. His restless mind wove the cloth in many different ways through the night, as Bullock snored unconcerned by his side. Just as dawn broke through the unglazed window of their shabby bedchamber, he dozed off. His dream was of wandering down endless passageways in the King's residence, desperately trying to reweave the opulent tapestries draped on the walls, which all fell into unconnected strands at his feet.

Brother John Darby awoke early and hurried through his morning prayers at prime. He chose to excuse himself from the daily meeting in the chapter house where rules were read and the daily administration of the abbey settled. The morning light was bright and clear, and he wanted to spend as much time as he could in the Scriptorium today. There was much to record in the Oseney Abbey Chronicles, and he had let enough time elapse for the events of the year so far to form a coherent whole. The news of the death of Pope Alexander was the culminating factor in his decision to note down a few succinct and considered sentences in the vast tome he kept always on his personal desk.

He scurried across the open courtyard that a few days earlier had been the scene of the students' despicable behaviour. The day felt fresh and the sun glinted off the streams and pools that were scattered across the low water-meadows between the abbey and the walls of Oxford. It was so early that a little mist was rising from the open meadow, and Brother John had the fanciful notion that the abbey was somehow set adrift from the harsh world of the common crowd inhabiting the city. He smiled, and wondered whether he would miss the outside world if the abbey was truly set adrift from it, to sail through paradise.

Climbing the stairs to his own personal domain of the Scriptorium, he shook his head ruefully to clear the foolish ideas from his mind. He had spent so long in observing and recording the world and its events, he could hardly abandon it now. Especially when some were predicting the Millennium. His footsteps echoed across the floor of the empty room as he walked through the dust motes sparkling in the sunlight from the high windows. He liked to be already at work when the monk-copyists in his charge arrived. It set them a good example, and pandered to what little vanity he possessed.

Stepping up to the raised dais that was his place of work, he opened the heavy leather-bound tome that lay permanently on his desk top. The outer surface of the book was smooth and shiny where his hands and those of his predecessors had caressed it lovingly. The work inevitably began with the Creation, and Brother John Darby was the third monk to carry on the recording of history for the abbey. He fancied he was the most accurate, especially as he insisted on being the only person to summarize each year as it occurred. His predecessors had let several hands make the summaries of yearly events. He turned to the back of the tome and withdrew the loose pages on which he was making the notes for 1261. He briefly scanned those he had already made.

'Louis, the oldest son of the King of France, is reported dead.'

Next to this there was a note in the margin reminding him to verify the exact date. He read on.

'The quarrel continues between King Henry and the barons because he refuses to observe the Provisions of Oxford. On Ash Wednesday terrible lightning and thunder was heard at Westminster.'

He carefully selected a new quill, and cut the end to a bold wedge. The ink on the desk had already been freshly mixed by the novice whose duty it was to precede even Brother John's arrival. The youth carried out his duties immediately after matins while the sky was still dark. Dipping the quill into the ink, he paused for a moment to gather his thoughts, then wrote after the last words, cutting confident black shapes into the creamy paper.

'Pope Alexander IV is dead. A dispute broke out at Oseney between the Papal Legate and some students. The Legate's brother has been killed and the students imprisoned at Wallingford.'

He paused, then in the margin scrawled himself another note. It read simply, '*Falconer?*'

The person in question was now on his way back to Oxford in the company of a refreshed Peter Bullock. Falconer was tired and irritable, and each stumble of the horse on the pitted road caused him to curse. Bullock thought he was perhaps jealous of the constable's effective interrogation of the warden. Falconer did so like to take the lead in their investigations. But Bullock fancied he knew his man, and the results with the warden had proved it. He was not going to apologize.

As they passed the point where yesterday they had turned off for Abingdon, Falconer heaved a great sigh and reined his horse in. Aghast, Bullock thought they were once again to embark on a wild-goose chase. But before he could remonstrate, Falconer spoke up.

'I am sorry for being so taciturn, my friend. It's so difficult to weave the strands together and come up with a satisfactory picture.'

Bullock was not sure what his comrade was talking about, but knew better than to interrupt him. He merely grunted an acknowledgement. They continued their journey side by side, and as the horses plodded at a pace to suit the constable's docile mount, Falconer explained what he had discovered as the greater truths so far.

Assuming that the Welshman had fired the shot, something that Bullock would have avowed as fact not assumption (but then he was keeping quiet), Falconer proposed the following theory. It was too much of a coincidence that this assault on the Bishop's life was brought about by a hot-headed student on the spur of the moment. There had already been several carefully planned assassination attempts and this had to be seen as another. The question was, who would wish to kill the Bishop and why? He was the representative of the Pope – and more than that, a candidate for the Papacy at a time when all knew the Pope was dying. Who in general condemned the venality and opulence of the Papacy? (Bullock would have said most English landowners and clerics seeking preferment.) Falconer supplied his own answer – the Dominicans. Who in the order had most recently expressed his views on what should happen to the Pope in the coming Apocalypse? (Bullock did not know, for he had not seen the Friar Preacher.) Again Falconer supplied the answer – Friar Robert Fordam.

Bullock could restrain himself no longer.

'The Welshman still pulled the bow string and loosed the arrow, not the friar.'

Falconer's face lit up with a huge smile of satisfaction.

'That's where you're wrong. The Welshman was just as much a weapon in the friar's hands as the bow was in his own.'

The constable shook his head in bewilderment, and Falconer continued to explain. He summarized the theory of the waking trance as expounded by his friend, Roger Bacon. It was his conviction that the friar used the technique when he preached, and he spoke of the people in London he had seen under the spell of Fordam. Falconer had seen the same look in the eyes of John Gryffin on his way to Oseney Abbey. Clearly the Welshman had been entranced into shooting an arrow at the Bishop when he emerged to see the students. Unfortunately, matters had gone awry when first the Bishop had refused to see the students, and secondly the Bishop's own brother (with a close family resemblance) had appeared with fatal consequences for himself.

The two men were now approaching Grandpont over the Thames and the city walls of Oxford were in sight. Falconer eased his aching back and finished off the weaving of events as he saw them. It only remained for the friar to kill John Gryffin and to make it look like a self-inflicted death in order to tidy up the whole affair. Perhaps the friar had aimed to do his killing in Oxford, but had happened upon the removal of his intended victim by the soldiers. So why not go with them? The figure Bullock had seen accompanying the soldiers and student-prisoners out of Oxford must have been Fordam. Who would have objected to a spiritual comfort for the poor youths? It only remained to place the friar in Wallingford yesterday.

'And that I intend to do today. Of course, there are still one or two little problems that don't add up.'

Falconer let a small frown cross his features.

'But I am sure I can explain them logically.'

Aethelmar, the Archbishop of Winchester, was resting after a tiring journey from London to Abingdon. Pursuing his half-brother, the King, around the country seemed to occupy most of his waking life. And his overweight frame was not designed to sit for many hours on the back of a horse. Well padded he might be, but the journeys on England's awful roads always made him bone-weary. He longed for the warmth of Provence, but politics prevented his return. He was obliged to remain in Henry's wet and windy domain, and even the current spell of dry days had not endeared the land to him. He supposed he should be grateful to his sister-in-law, the Queen, for obtaining him his lucrative position, but he could not bring himself to be thankful for second best.

While he always seemed to be one step behind his half-brother geographically, now perhaps he could get ahead of him politically – and provide himself with the leverage to remain in his post, when all around him his fellow countrymen were being forced out by the barons of England, led by that renegade Frenchman, Simon de Montfort. Aethelmar had been quick to see the value of having the King and the Papal Legate in the same place. How many times had he tried to broker alliances, only to have the King load his baggage on wagons and leave before the other party could speak to him? Even here, the King could strike out in any direction. From Abingdon, roads led to Woodstock and Tewkesbury, Wallingford and Windsor, and Marlborough, whence he could travel to Winchester, Salisbury or Bristol. In a few days, he could be anywhere in his kingdom collecting his taxes and living off his subjects. He had to act fast in pushing Henry towards a decision on Otho and the papal contest.

He decided to arrange a meeting as soon as decently possible. In the meantime he needed to get a message to Segrim and the others of his faction, so they could silence the rumours about the death in Oxford immediately. It would not do for inquisitive meddlers to arouse the suspicions of the Bishop.

The sun was already setting when Falconer returned through Little Gate after a fruitless interview with the head of the Dominican order in Oxford. Falconer had been at first distracted by the old man's pale and strained appearance, but had been reassured by details of the treatment he was receiving. He much respected old Richard de Sotell. In spite of his attitude towards the Jews, he was in all other matters a man of learning. He was also canny, and had not given away anything about Robert Fordam's whereabouts.

This last frustration had come on a day of frustrations. After the journey back from Wallingford, Falconer had hurriedly stabled the borrowed horses, only to find himself embroiled in a dispute with a neighbouring hall over the conduct of his students the previous night. It would appear he could not trust them to behave themselves in his absence. Drunkenness and high spirits could be excused, but not when they resulted in the singeing of a valuable book. Naturally Hugh Pett claimed they were merely trying to set light to the purse of a particularly tight-fisted Scottish clerk to teach him a lesson. It was not their fault that the purse, still round the Scot's waist at the time, had also held a copy of Priscian's *Grammar*. Falconer had had to compensate the Scot, and vowed that the culprits would go hungry for a week to recoup the lost money.

This had delayed his pursuit of Friar Fordam, and his interview with the Friar-Senior had got him no more than an assurance Fordam was not in the friary. Still, the thought occurred to him that Fordam could not be far away, and would have to return to the friary soon. He decided that, despite the late hour, he would wait at Little Gate to see if Fordam came by. At this hour, the physical danger from nightwalkers usually prevented honest citizens from being abroad. However, the Regent Master was used to late-night walks to soothe his often racing brain, and he depended on his size and presence to deter any would-be robbers.

There was a narrow alley just north of the gateway. It led to Beef Hall and Falconer settled himself in the doorway of the hall, close to the corner of the lane. From there he could see Little Gate and was protected from the cold evening breeze that whistled down the alley. The city's gates were normally locked at night, but Falconer knew the Dominicans had a key to this gate, which led on to their island on the Thames. If Fordam was in the city, he would come this way.

In the end, Falconer did not have long to wait, for which he was grateful. He had underestimated the drop in temperature this cool spring evening. The gloomy alley had lost the sunlight early, and the iron rivets studding the door pierced his clothes like spears of ice. His thin shoes did little to protect him from the freezing slab of stone under his feet. Just as he was thinking of moving in order to warm up, the oak door of Little Gate creaked. Falconer blinked. Surely he had not dozed off and missed Fordam leaving through the gate? Then he realized the door was not closing but being hesitantly opened. Someone was entering the city. Falconer was disappointed at first – the slight, habit-clad figure was clearly not that of Friar Robert Fordam. The fresh face that turned towards him, after the friar relocked the gate, confirmed that. It was full of apprehension at being in such a dangerous place. Then Falconer realized this young novice would not be abroad on his own initiative. He must have been sent by de Sotell, probably to find Friar Fordam. If he followed the youth, he might find his quarry.

But first he pressed himself even further into the rough wooden timbers of the doorway he was using to spy from. The young Dominican was walking straight towards him. He held his breath and prayed the youth's eyesight was as bad as his own. Fortunately the friar scurried past, intent on reaching the safer open space of Pennyfarthing Street. Giving him a few seconds' start, Falconer emerged from his hiding-place and peered cautiously round the edge of the building. The figure of the Dominican was already turning right at the top of the lane, and Falconer hurried to keep up with him.

Reaching the wider street himself, Falconer turned in the same direction and followed in the shadows. The Dominican crossed the main street leading to South Gate, and hurried up to the door of the building opposite. It was the House of Converts, endowed by Henry III to accommodate those unfortunate Jewish souls who were harried into adopting Christianity. Their conversion effectively rendered them destitute, as they could no longer practise usury and were barred from the support of their former family and friends. They spent their miserable days learning handicrafts and were totally dependent on charity. If that was where Fordam was, Falconer was not surprised – he could envisage the friar taking the opportunity to gloat over the misfortune of others.

He stayed at the entrance of the street opposite and kept his eyes on the doors of the house. A few minutes after the young novice had entered, the doors were flung open and Fordam emerged, with the young man in frightened pursuit. Falconer just had time to dive through an archway leading into the precincts of St Aldate's Church before the two Dominicans flew past him, their sandals slapping on the hard earth. He followed their hasty flight back towards Little Gate, and called out as the young novice fumbled with the key to the door.

The older man turned around, prepared to defend himself from attack, then recognized the man in drab but obviously clerical garb. It was the Master who had snatched the young seeker for truth away from him yesterday. He looked back at the fearful novice, and asked for the key. Once the trembling youth had given it to him, he told him to return to the friary and said he would lock the gate himself. He waited until the youth had disappeared through the dark archway and into the night, then turned his glaring eyes on Falconer.

'I would guess you are the Master Falconer, about whom Friar Richard sent the warning.'

'That is my name. But why do you need to be warned about someone who is merely seeking a little truth?'

'Truth? You are no truth-seeker. Your actions at this very

gate yesterday betray you as a hider from the truth, who is destined for the sulphurous pit.'

Falconer snorted.

'Spare me the harangue. I heard it in London and it did not impress me then. The Lord will make his Last Judgement in his own time. Your sort were predicting the end of the world after a thousand years of our Lord's rule. And no doubt you'll still be predicting it after two thousand years.'

Falconer expected the other man to explode at this, but strangely he didn't. Fordam merely stood calmly in the open doorway of Little Gate, gently swinging the key he held in his right hand. As he spoke, Falconer was more aware of the soothing tone of his voice than what he was actually saying. The soft light of the moon sparkled from the swinging key in the friar's hand, and his eyes were drawn to it. He began to wonder why he had been so angry, and felt more relaxed than he had done since the death at Oseney Abbey. The friar was beckoning him to follow through the open gate, and Falconer could see no reason not to acquiesce. The stars seemed so bright through the archway and the prospect beyond so inviting. He had forgotten entirely about the icy wind that blew down the narrow alleys between the houses.

He stood counting the stars as the friar locked the gate behind them. The friar's voice liltingly drew him along. He seemed to be floating as he followed the friar along the enticing track that led – where? He could not recall, but it seemed so alluring. The friar led him to a grassy bank and encouraged him to lie down. It seemed so cool and comfortable, and he dropped to his knees. He felt so tired and in need of rest, and the bank was so soft. He put his hands down and they seemed to push through the downy surface of the bank.

'Enough!'

The harsh voice cut like a knife into Falconer's brain, and he suddenly felt cold. He looked down and realized he was kneeling in the icy waters of Trill Mill stream. His robes were soaked. He shuddered and snatched at the gnarled hand that was thrust down at him. Richard de Sotell helped him out of the bottom of the ditch, and Falconer gained the top of the grassy bank gasping. If he had lain down in the water, he did not doubt he could have drowned, even though it was only shallow.

Friar Fordam hovered behind his Friar-Senior, his face like thunder, but evidently cowed. Falconer still felt bereft of control over his own actions, and just stood shivering, water dripping from his soaked clothes. It was de Sotell who broke the awkward silence.

'Come, you will freeze here. I have a warm fire in my room at the friary. Anyway, you deserve an explanation.'

Chapter Eight

Waking up the following morning safe in his own chamber at Aristotle's Hall, Falconer could almost have imagined that the events of the previous night had not taken place. But, sitting up in bed, he saw his robe from yesterday hanging over the back of his solitary chair, a pool of water underneath it. Falconer rose and doused his fuddled head in a bowl of cold water left inside the door by one of his students. As the water dripped off his face, he was reminded of last night – a night that might have been his last. He rubbed some life back into his cold features with a piece of coarse sacking. Only when his cheeks glowed with the rough treatment did he feel he was truly awake.

The papers sent by Bacon still stared at him from the table. On the top of the stack was the handful of sentences on the waking trance. He now had first-hand experience of its reality. Could Friar Fordam have used the technique on John Gryffin to induce him to attempt to kill the Bishop? Richard de Sotell had tried to convince him last night that he could not. He did not think that anyone could be forced to act against their natural instincts so totally as to kill. Even by someone with the skill of Robert Fordam. Falconer had insisted that he himself had nearly died, thanks to that skill. The old man was sceptical that, when it came to resting his face in the water, Falconer would have continued, even in a trance. Whatever might have happened, he gave thanks to God that the young novice had had the good sense to report back to the Friar-Senior. His anxious search for Falconer and Fordam had meant that Fordam's powers had not been put to the ultimate test.

Still Falconer clung on to his theory of Fordam's culpability. He just needed to be able to show that the preaching friar could have been in Wallingford at the right time, and could have had the opportunity to entrance John Gryffin prior to the murder of Sinibaldo. At first de Sotell's words had given Falconer some sort of optimism.

'I cannot say where he was before the death of the Bishop's man. He was travelling, and was first seen on the streets of Oxford the following day, preaching in the market. Yes, he could have been here the day of the murder and could have met John Gryffin.'

Falconer grunted with satisfaction. But then the old man continued.

'But I still have not seen his entrancement make someone act contrary to their nature. And after that first day, including the time you say the student was killed, Friar Fordam was always within the confines of the friary.'

It was at this point that Falconer's fine theories, expounded to Bullock on the journey back from Wallingford, had fallen apart. Fordam could not have been the mystery figure with the students when they were moved to Wallingford. Nor could he have been present at the castle in order to commit the murder. From the time he had returned from London until last night, Fordam had been undertaking a penance for de Sotell. He had been under the Friar-Senior's eyes at all times, and had been released only that evening to assist at the House of Converts. He simply had not had the time to get to Wallingford and back. The penance had been imposed for preaching the Apocalypse too vehemently, and because de Sotell had become worried about his influence over people's actions. His use of those powers over Falconer had now convinced de Sotell to put him securely in a solitary cell in the far north of England, where he might ponder on his errant ways. The friar would shortly make his journey thence. That was the end of Falconer's fine theory.

Falconer now knew he had to seek other truths. He had to

admit to having been seduced by Friar Bacon's records to the exclusion of the facts before him. He tidied the stack of Bacon's precious papers and stowed them in his clothes chest on top of his meagre collection of robes. They would be undisturbed there.

His next step was to return to what he knew. His only other suspect for the murder of John Gryffin was Humphrey Segrim, who at least had been present at Oseney Abbey when the master cook had been killed. And at Wallingford Castle. The mystery accomplice dressed as a friar or monk would have to wait. He should clearly pursue the main offender. Anyway, with Fordam eliminated, Falconer had no other avenue to explore. He resolved to interview Segrim and, feeling refreshed by the possibility of a new line of investigation, resolved to do it the moment he had completed his morning lecture.

The weather was unusually mild, and Falconer chose to walk the few miles to Botley. He was heartily sick of sitting astride a horse, and knew he could revive himself with a vigorous walk across the water-meadows. Passing the walls of Oseney Abbey, he restrained the temptation to enter and enquire of Brother John about the progress on copying the Aristotle. He would be patient. Soon he was crossing the Seacourt stream at the bridge that led to Botley and Humphrey Segrim's imposing manor house. Stooping down, he cupped his hands and drank a draught of the cool water to ease the dry tickle in his throat he put down to the dust of the track. As he rose, he heard the distant bell of the abbey toll sext, the middle of the day.

The house stood on a small rise, a substantial timber-frame building sitting on solid stone, with a tower on the east side for defence. As he approached the small moat that encircled the house, he looked through the arch of the walled garden that stood beside the lane. He saw a young woman stooped over the plants, engrossed in her selection. He felt moved to stop, and as he stood in the archway, she must have become aware of his presence. She looked up and coolly returned his stare. Alas, he was too far away to see the detail of her features with his poor eyes, but her shape was more than pleasing to him. From the self-assured way she returned his gaze, he presumed she must be Segrim's wife and not a servant. He would have sought to make her acquaintance but a voice from behind broke into his thoughts.

'Master Falconer. What do you want here?'

Falconer turned round to discover Humphrey Segrim astride a powerful horse of dimensions greater than any nag the Regent Master had ever hired. Segrim's superior manner was further emphasized by his lofty perch. But Falconer was not intimidated.

'Could we talk about the students imprisoned at Wallingford?'

'You'd better come inside.'

Segrim threw his response over his shoulder as he spurred the horse up the dusty lane. He didn't offer the horse's broad back to Falconer, who was obviously expected to make his own way to the house. Falconer waited for the dust to settle, and turned with a wry grin to the young woman. But she had already returned to the collecting of herbs.

The hall of Segrim's manor house was cool and gloomy after the brightness of the spring day. Shafts of light speared in from the high windows, but did not penetrate to the central hearth, where Segrim stood poking through the cold ashes with his booted foot. Falconer came straight to the point.

'I believe you escorted the students to Wallingford.'

'I would not say escorted. That was the duty of the King's men. I did precede them to Wallingford. On the King's business.'

'You know that one of them is now dead, of course.'

Falconer could not tell whether the look of surprise on Segrim's face was real or feigned.

'How did he die?'

'He was found hanged.'

Segrim seemed to have regained his composure, and continued

his careful sifting of the ashes with the toe of his boot.

'So the young Welshman killed himself. A sure sign of guilt, I would have thought.'

'That's what we are being led to believe.'

Falconer's remark once again caused Segrim to stop his prodding of the ashes and look with curiosity at the Regent Master. There was a movement behind Falconer, but as he turned, he saw it was just a servant scurrying about his duties. He caught himself half wishing it had been Segrim's wife. The other man continued.

'Is that not what you believe? Not that the opinions of a Regent Master of the University have any relevance in this case.'

'I believe what the facts tell me.' Falconer's reply was cryptic enough to allow Segrim to believe what he wished. He seemed satisfied by the response and was about to usher Falconer out, when the Regent Master realized what Segrim had said earlier. He cursed himself for having been distracted by thoughts of the man's wife. Stopping the smooth progress to the door, he asked Segrim another question.

'How did you know it was the Welshman who had died?'

'The Welshman?'

'You said the young Welshman hanged himself. I didn't tell you which student had died.'

Segrim thought for a moment.

'I suppose I assumed it was him. When the students arrived at the castle, he was morose where the others were a disorderly bunch. They all thought that someone was going to save them, young fools. He thought otherwise, and looked on the verge of killing himself even then. I told the warden to put him in a separate cell. I didn't tell him to leave the youth with the means of taking his own life. Now you must leave. I have important visitors.'

Falconer was far from satisfied but allowed himself to be ushered back into the sunlight. Returning down the track, he stopped at the arch of the herb garden, but Segrim's wife was no longer there. On a whim he ventured through the arch and smelled the plants the woman had been picking. He crushed some rosemary to release the scent and sneezed. By chance, he was therefore out of sight when Segrim's 'important visitors' started arriving. It gave him the opportunity to observe them and they were a strange mixture indeed.

The first he saw was on foot, and was clearly Brother Peter Talam, the hood of his habit thrown back due to the warm weather. His curiosity piqued, Falconer resolved to hide in the garden a little longer. He brushed through the luxuriant growth of herbs and stood in the shade cast by the high, encircling wall. After a while he began to shiver, and was about to give up on his foolish idea when he heard the thunder of hooves in the lane. He stood close to the archway and strained his eyes, but the four horsemen were past too swiftly for him to be able to recognize anyone. One was fat and sat astride his mount uncomfortably, where the others were lean and used to a life in the saddle. They passed in a blur of rich colours and were no doubt men of substance, apart from one man in sober garb, whose horse strove to keep up with the others. Him aside, the men rode chargers that were large and draped in cloth emblazoned with coats of arms. Segrim was indeed moving in noble circles. There was much here to ponder on, but for now Falconer would have to return to Oxford.

Outside the wall, another pair of eyes, stronger than Falconer's, had also witnessed the comings and goings. De Beaujeu's stalking of the Regent Master was proving invaluable for many reasons.

The lady of Botley Manor had rushed from the herb garden to the kitchens with her harvest. There, she was just in time to eavesdrop on the conversation between her husband and the man who had stared so calmly at her from the archway of the walled garden. She already knew his name as Falconer, for Humphrey had called it out in the lane. Now she knew he was a Regent Master at Oxford University, and that he had a great interest in her husband's affairs. The latter meant he was of great interest to her. Perhaps they could be of mutual benefit at some point. She could not imagine, however, where the death of a student fitted in.

She waited in the kitchen until her husband led the Master out, fussing over the meal the cook was preparing. Just as she was about to enter the hall, she heard horses arriving in the courtyard, and the voice of her husband summoning the servants to take care of them. He had not told her there would be any more visitors, so she assumed this meeting must be a secret. Eager to learn more, she stood close behind the heavy drape that separated the kitchens from the hall. She was rewarded with an insight into the nature of the conspiracy in which her husband was involved.

Indeed she need not have hidden – he did not even look to see if they could be overheard. She pitied the other men for being linked with her husband, who clearly lacked the skill to keep a conspiracy quiet. At best he assumed his wife was too naive or dutiful to take an interest, at worst he had forgotten she was present. She risked a glance around the edge of the arras.

The group of men were huddled around the central hearth, even though there was no fire. Occasionally one would leap up and pace around, waving his arms to emphasize a point. They were all self-assured men, each wanting his own opinions to hold sway. One, tall and heavily bearded with thick silver hair, seemed to be winning the day. He was supported by a soberly dressed man who seemed out of place, a man of letters in the company of men of action.

Ann could not hear everything that was said, but what she did hear astonished her, reaching as it did beyond the shores of the realm – to the very heart of the Church in Rome. She also heard disparaging remarks made about the King, whom the group professed to serve. His obsession with the rebuilding of Westminster Abbey as a shrine to Edward the Confessor was mocked, especially as it took funds away from the purpose in hand.

'It is said on good evidence that Henry no longer sleeps with his wife, but with the Confessor's remains at his side.'

This grisly remark from the silver-haired man had the group in fits of laughter, as did a retort from Segrim.

'I always thought his son was a bag of bones.'

Eventually the laughter subsided, and the conversation became hushed as the men once again put their heads together over the cold hearth. Ann could hear no more, and was about to slip away to avoid discovery, when she heard the name of her husband's previous visitor. Why were they interested in Master Falconer? She risked another glance around the arras.

The soberly dressed man was speaking.

'Leave him to me. I am sure I can convince him that you were not involved in the death at the abbey.'

The others nodded agreement and the meeting began to break up. Ann slipped quietly back into the kitchen and out through the rear door. She took deep breaths of fresh air, to rid her system of the stink of conspiracy and self-serving.

Thomas de Cantilupe was a little nervous of his meeting with Regent Master Falconer. He knew the man by reputation from stories provided by his predecessor in the Chancellorship. The man was obviously a nuisance and a freethinker, who would need to be kept under control – removed if possible, especially if de Cantilupe's higher political ambitions were to be achieved. The Chancellor-elect had been surprised and flattered when Segrim had asked him to share in secret work for the King. Indeed this involvement seemed a good first step for him towards becoming known directly to the King. His first meeting with the group of nobles at Botley Manor had gone well. To be in the company of such highly placed men as Gilbert de Clare and Bishop Aethelmar was flattering. However, he was uncertain about the noble lords' irreverent attitude to Henry. And he sometimes felt that unspoken messages were passing from one member of the group to another, which specifically left him out. Still, he reasoned that he would have to prove himself to them before he was taken fully into their confidence.

Perhaps that was why he was wary of Master Falconer. This was his first test as a valuable member of the clique. If Falconer was intent on pursuing the question of the death in the Papal Legate's entourage, he would ensure he did not waste time badgering people who were serving the King. The matter was silly anyway. Was it not obvious that the unfortunate Welshman had killed the man? Better still, he should stop Falconer wasting his time on any sort of investigation, now and in the future. The man had plenty to occupy him teaching students.

Falconer was wondering what the new Chancellor was going to be like. With his predecessor, he had been able to avoid any censure despite his constant involvement in various 'little problems'. At Chancellor's Court, the old man had it within his powers to banish Falconer beyond the limits of the town, or to fine him, either of which would have been ruinous. Usually, the Regent Master's persistent justification of his actions had resulted in the Chancellor being grateful to get Falconer out of his sight and the range of his ears. Now he would have to learn how to conduct himself with this new man, who was not yet even installed as Chancellor.

He was led into de Cantilupe's presence by Halegod, the same old, stooped figure who had served the previous Chancellor – and no doubt the Chancellor before him, judging from his wrinkled face and rheumy eyes. He seemed to be a permanent fixture, along with the fading tapestries that kept out the draughts from the Chancellor's private rooms.

De Cantilupe sat behind a large trestle table spread with the remains of his dinner. He was fond of good food and wine, though in other matters he was an ascetic, and had not allowed his hurried return to Oxford and summoning of Falconer to delay his repast. He fingered the crumbs of his trencher, and absently popped a lump into his mouth. He could still taste the rich, spicy stew he had sopped up with the bread. He decided to stay seated where he was and spread his hands, palms down, on the table in what he fondly imagined to be a posture of power.

From behind the table he surveyed the large, rangy man in front of him. He was clad in a worn clerical robe which had once been black, but now had faded to dark green. The man's bony hands protruded from his sleeves which ended in frayed edges several inches above his wrists. His weather-beaten face was topped with grizzled hair. He was most unlike the average Regent Master who was either young and fresh-faced, or old and pasty-looking. What was more startling were the man's eyes. They were pale, cornflower blue and seemed to pierce to de Cantilupe's soul. He shifted on his seat.

For Falconer's part, he saw a thin-visaged man whose face was dominated by a hooked Roman nose that split it into two. His flushed, veiny cheeks suggested a fondness for the wines of France, and the scattered remains of a prodigious meal in front of him betokened a man who accompanied his wine with good food. The eyes that surveyed him were hooded, and burned with naked ambition. Falconer looked forward to a good contest with a worthy adversary.

De Cantilupe found himself rising to meet the other man, as though drawn to him as an equal. Irritated at his involuntary act, he nevertheless gave in to the inevitable and circled the table, picking up a large flagon as he did so. He called out to Halegod to bring another wine cup. If the man could not be faced down with authority, de Cantilupe would win him over with comradeship. He poured himself a generous draught of the Guienne, and took the other cup from Halegod who had scuttled into the room, startled at de Cantilupe's unaccustomed generosity with his best wine. He poured out the rest of the wine and handed it to Falconer, motioning him into a chair on the opposite side of the unlit fireplace. He sat in the other chair which was artfully placed to avoid draughts from both door and window. The evening was overcast, and the unglazed windows furnished no light, only a blast of air that shifted the ashes in the fireplace in circular patterns. De Cantilupe was clad in several layers of clothes, including a hair shirt that offered warmth as well as the discomfort of humility. He knew the other chair provided his guests with an icy sensation from the feet up. No one could tell whether that came from his lofty presence or from the winds that blew through the Chancellor's residence. Feeling more in control of the meeting, he settled himself down, took a deep swig of good Guienne and made inconsequential enquiries about Falconer's students.

Falconer waited for the opening salvo, knowing the pleasantries the Chancellor-elect was offering were only the preliminaries. Seeing the man lean forward in his seat, he knew the important point had been reached. He could not even look Falconer in the eye – the matter must be serious.

Gazing deep into his empty wine cup, de Cantilupe broached the subject of the murder.

'I have heard that you have involved yourself in unexplained deaths in the city in the past.'

Falconer merely acknowledged the fact with a stare.

'I can understand your keenness to demonstrate the application of logic to practical matters. But isn't murder rather a mundane affair, best left to those of a . . .' He paused, seeking the right word. '. . . physical bent? Logic should be utilized in the resolution of more lofty issues.'

'Such as how the first Eucharist was celebrated while Christ's body was in the grave,' snorted Falconer.

De Cantilupe was shocked at the Regent Master's scorn of a crucial religious debate. Nevertheless, he pursued his main point.

'Take the matter of the unfortunate Welshman. It is clear he shot the arrow that killed the Bishop's brother. It is equally clear he took his own life in remorse. What more is there to say on the subject?'

Falconer seized the opening that the incautious Chancellor had given him.

'There is much to seek out, and then more to say. There would have been little to say if the Welshman had indeed hanged himself.

But the truths tell me otherwise. John Gryffin was murdered, and so I must ask myself why. Not by the authorities that held him. So, by whom? We could assume an accomplice to the first murder from amongst the other students. One who wished to save his own neck. But then, why was he killed after the students had been separated? So much easier to arrange his apparent suicide while he occupies the same cell than when there are two locked doors between you and your victim.'

Falconer leaned forward eagerly, finding his own thoughts clarifying as he spoke. The Chancellor-elect sat gloomily in his seat, unable to stop the flow, and realizing his words had had the opposite effect to that he desired.

'No, the Welshman's murder confirms the existence of an accomplice, or perhaps a controlling hand. And it would have to be someone outside the circle of students. Someone with a greater reason to kill the Bishop than his laughing about a scalded beggar. It becomes a grander matter, concerning the papal power and succession. And involves grander men than a few ragged students. I begin to wonder at whose behest the arrow was let fly. Who was present at the death of both the Bishop's brother and John Gryffin?

'The answer is Humphrey Segrim.'

The Chancellor-elect saw his whole future slipping away from him. His power and influence were great but limited to the University. He had wider ambitions and needed the support of the King. Segrim was his link with Henry, so Falconer's statement caused cold tremors to shoot down his spine.

The man was indeed off on a wild-goose chase, but one dangerously close to home. But de Cantilupe could not rein in Falconer's thinking now.

'And who does Segrim work for? Who is powerful enough to want the Papal Legate out of the way? Why, the King himself.'

The words were out of Falconer's mouth almost before the thought had entered his head. De Cantilupe rose from his chair, beads of sweat standing out on his brow despite the cold room. He turned his back on Falconer and paced up the room. Falconer was about to mention the lordly conspirators he had seen arriving at Segrim's house yesterday, when he suddenly realized who the more soberly dressed figure riding in their wake had been. De Cantilupe was one of them.

The Fifth Seal

In the year 1250, Louis, King of France, began his attack on the Saracens. He had received absolution and blessing from the Pope two years before, upon committing himself to the Crusade. Having landed in Egypt, Louis decided to cross the river called Thanis on Ash Wednesday. Some Templars and other noblemen crossed before him and were exposed to the great host of the heathen army. The King could not come to their help, for he too was surrounded by Saracens. In the battle fought on that day there perished most of the knights of the Temple, William Longspee, Raoul de Coucy, the Count of Artois and many other Christians. In retreat the King himself was captured, suffering from an evil sickness. When the Fifth Seal was broken there was revealed underneath the altar the souls of those who were martyred for God's word. Each of them was given a white robe, and asked to rest a while until all who were to be killed in God's service had joined them.

From the *Chronica Oseneiensis*

Chapter Nine

The prime bell calling the monks of Oseney Abbey to early Mass could be heard in the manor of Botley. Ann Segrim was already dressed in a long, flowing robe of red, bound tight at her slim waist. She had chosen the dress of light material because it emphasized her shape, and it would help her in what she sought to do today. She sat arranging her hair under the fashionable net that she wore to display her thick blonde tresses. She hated to hide her locks under a wimple.

She looked at herself in the mirror that her husband had bought her in the days when he sought to win her favours. The clear silver glass enclosed in a wooden frame with a horn handle was a rarity in England, and Ann treasured it even though Humphrey had expected a night in her bed in return. She smiled at her own image, the unlined face of a mature woman who could still attract the attention of men. The thought of the Regent Master who had stared at her in the garden passed through her mind. She made her mirror image frown at her in censure. After all, she was a married woman.

On the other hand, she might see him in Oxford today, and a chance meeting could prove fortuitous in her search for the truth about her husband's activities. But her first stop was Oseney Abbey, where she wanted to talk to the monk who had visited her husband yesterday. She knew his name was Talam and that he was the bursar of the abbey. Perhaps she could discover more about her husband's affairs by drawing him out with talk of a donation? Or should she essay the innocent application of her female attractions?

She left her chamber quietly so as not to disturb Humphrey. But when she heard the loud snoring emanating from his room, she tripped more happily down the staircase, the folds of her red robe held high and revealing her ankles. The servant had her horse ready in the yard, together with his own skinny nag. Having assisted her to mount, he clambered on the quivering wreck that was all Humphrey Segrim allowed him and prayed it would survive the journey. The lady Ann was already through the archway and down the road before he had forced the nag into a trot. Not that this mattered too much, for as they travelled he knew to keep at a discreet distance behind his mistress. She liked to think herself free and alone on her rare trips to the city.

The master had been advised that his wife was going to Oxford to select a brooch from the goldsmiths who plied their trade in the shops beneath the Golden Cross Inn. Sekston did not know if that was the true reason or if she had a tryst with another man, and he preferred not to know. It would not be safe to be the conveyor of the news to his master that he was a cuckold. His position depended on being blind, deaf and dumb to his betters' antics at all times.

Peter Bullock could not remember when he had first become suspicious. In a town the size of Oxford, thousands of people passed in front of his eyes. Even so, he was bound to see the same faces time and again in his regular patrols through the narrow lanes. But this face seemed to crop up at particular times in particular places. The man was tall and well built, and his confident manner gave Bullock the impression he was a soldier by trade. His face was tanned, as though he had spent time away from the dull skies and soft sunlight of England and France. His short tunic revealing muscular legs only confirmed him as a man of action.

Only yesterday, Bullock had become aware of the man apparently following in the footsteps of his friend, William Falconer, as he hurried out of his morning lectures. Even then he had spotted him only because he seemed a little out of place in Schools Lane amongst all the young students. As Bullock watched on with interest, the man had followed Falconer down to the High Street.

There he had dogged his footsteps as the Regent Master turned west. Bullock had followed both of them to be certain that he was not mistaken. The man might simply have been walking in the same direction. Falconer had left the city through the little-used postern gate under St George's Tower, and his shadow had paused long enough to ensure he was not too close once in open countryside, and gone through also. Bullock marvelled at his ability to merge with his surroundings.

For the rest of the day, the man's appearance niggled at something in Bullock's memory, and he began to imagine he had seen him in all sorts of places. Had it been in the market, emerging from St Frideswide's Church one evening, and near his own courtyard below the Great Keep? He even thought he might have passed him on the road to Wallingford Castle. Having completed his solitary supper, he tried to put the whole idea out of his mind as ludicrous, and slumped into the narrow cot that was his bed. The exposed planks that formed its base usually eased him off to sleep, as they reminded him of nights spent on hard earth as a foot soldier. He had once tried to sleep on a soft mattress filled with straw, but had eventually thrown it out. His body was used to more spartan conditions and he could not retrain it now.

That night the planks seemed full of knots and bumps that dug into his flesh, and the mysterious man haunted his brain. Even the first light of day over the top of the Great Keep did not disperse the image, and he finally decided that he had not been imagining the elusive man's presence. Everywhere William Falconer had gone, the man had been not far behind. Except in one particular instance. In the case of the Wallingford road he had been far ahead. Far enough to have entered the castle and killed John Gryffin before the arrival of the two friends. Bullock sat up in his cot and resolved to solve this mystery on his own, without the intervention of Master William Falconer. Today he would find the man again and discover who he was. Before he perhaps killed his friend.

At the same time that Ann Segrim was tripping past her snoring husband in Botley, Bullock rose from his cot and threw on his clothes. If he stationed himself near Aristotle's Hall, he stood a good chance of encountering the stranger – if the man really existed, and if he was in fact trailing Falconer. He lumbered through the quiet streets of Oxford, with the traders just stirring and lowering the shutters of their shops. He kept to the narrow lanes near the southern ramparts of the imposing city walls. This way he kept in the shadows with the watery sun barely warming the rooftops. As he passed St Frideswide's Church, he saw a figure ahead of him. Someone was turning down the lane that led to Falconer's hall, also keeping to the shadows. And Bullock knew who it was. A few moments sooner and he would have collided with the man he sought.

Following on more cautiously, he admired the quiet and flowing movements of his adversary. The man could probably walk right up to a deer in the forest without disturbing it. Bullock's heavy frame and bent back could never contrive to move so silently. So he kept well back, and was startled when the man seemed to disappear. Bullock paused, then stepped into a nearby doorway to think without being seen. As he did so, he realized the other man had done exactly the same. Now he was just a shadow in a shadow, waiting for the man he was stalking. And the constable would have to be patient in his turn.

As it turned out, neither the mystery man nor Bullock had long to wait. The lane soon filled with fresh-faced young men, jostling each other as they hurried to their lectures. Though one or two cast a curious eye on the constable pressed into his doorway, no one seemed to notice the other man. This was so evident that Bullock began to wonder if he had been wrong and the man was not there at all. In disgust at his foolishness, he stepped out into the lane and walked towards Aristotle's Hall. Before he had gone a few paces, he saw Falconer coming towards him, his drab black robe flapping around his ankles. He stopped to await his friend, and could scarcely disguise his surprise when the shadow man suddenly appeared behind the Regent Master.

Bullock stood his ground, and was about to hail his friend. But Falconer swept past him as though he hadn't seen the constable. There was an unusually serious expression on the Regent Master's face that clouded his normally alert blue eyes. His look suggested to Bullock a man deep in thought, and although he was annoyed by Falconer's lack of reaction, it suited his present situation. He moved on down the lane, as though his only intent was to ensure there was no trouble from the unruly students. He didn't dare give the shadow man even a sideways glance as he passed. Walking on until he was sure the followed and the follower were out of the lane, he stopped and turned cautiously round. He was relieved to see they were both out of sight.

He scuttled on to the other end of the lane and turned down the narrow alley that ran the length of Aristotle's Hall's eastern side. If he ran, he could intercept the procession as it crossed the High Street and discover what happened after the stranger had observed Falconer safely at his work again. He hurried round behind the crumbling edifice of St Mary's Church and was in time to see the back of the Regent Master disappearing into the room he used to take his students through their paces.

The man seemed resigned to the fact that Falconer was at his work and not going elsewhere. He stood at the doorway for a few moments, then shrugged his shoulders and turned back to the High Street. This time Bullock kept close enough not to lose him. The man strolled casually back to the Golden Cross Inn, and after a few minutes emerged from the inn yard on a charger that he spurred towards South Gate. The man carried no extra burden with him, so Bullock assumed he had not left permanently. He smiled in triumph. The man's departure would give him time to examine his baggage and discover something about him.

Ralph Harbottle, Abbot of Oseney, sat back on the stone bench that ran around the cloister and let the morning sun warm his old bones. At this time of the day the sun was low enough to penetrate the arches that spanned the passage round the outer edge of the square, where it would normally be shaded. As he got older, Ralph hated the cold and gloom of each English winter more. His aching limbs begged for warmth, and the other monks knew better than to disturb him on mornings such as these. Banishing the horror of creeping senility, Ralph recalled the time of his own novitiate, nearly forty years ago.

That was in the days of King Henry's minority, a handful of years after the death of John. Then the monks really did work for themselves, not as now. Now the abbey employed labourers to work the farm, and the monks led a life devoid of manual toil. It served only to emphasize the aphorism that the world was divided into three classes – those who fought, those who laboured, and those who prayed. As a novice he had risen soon after midnight and prayed in the chapter house until dawn, when the assembled monks attended prime. The rest of the morning had been taken up in manual labour until terce and another solemn ceremony. After a service and a meal at sext, there had been more manual work to carry out, followed by the sixth service of the day at nones. And he had been brought up on a meatless diet. Only the sick had then been allowed the flesh of other beasts. Now everyone, including himself, who took a fancy for the taste of meat presented themselves as being ill and resorted to the infirmary. Nothing of the old values lasted.

Seeing the old man dozing in the sun, Brother John Darby hesitated, but the visitor had asked to see the Abbot and he could not refuse. The lady Ann Segrim had arrived early at the gates of the abbey, accompanied only by a servant. Darby had chanced to be crossing the main courtyard on his way to the Scriptorium when she had dismounted from her horse. His sense of good fortune had not least been affected by the nature of the lady's dress, which clung to her figure in the light wind. He now led her into the presence of the Abbot, coughing circumspectly to rouse the old man.

More than the cough, the sweet scent of lavender woke Ralph Harbottle, incongruous as it was in this part of the abbey. Seeing the round, ruddy face of Brother John, he was about to castigate the monk for disturbing him when he realized the provenance of the errant scent. He recognized the comely woman with hair the colour of straw as the wife of Humphrey Segrim.

'Forgive me, Abbot, but this lady wishes to speak with you.'

Ralph sat up on the stone seat and arranged his robes around him, striving to bring his mind back to the present. He motioned for the woman to sit beside him and asked her what she wished to know. Brother John hovered anxiously in the shadow of the arches and Ralph noticed that the monk could not take his eyes off the shape of Ann Segrim. He had not really noticed her well-formed figure until that moment, and sadly supposed that was due to his age rather than his celibate resolve. He suddenly realized that the woman was speaking.

'I am sorry, child, I fear my mind was elsewhere. What is it you said?'

'Actually, it was Brother Talam that I wanted to see.' Her voice to Ralph's ears was light and sweet. 'On a monetary matter for my husband.'

Before Ralph could respond, Brother John stepped out of the shade, twisting the cord of his habit in his hands.

'If you will remember, Father, Brother Talam is unwell.'

The Abbot could not recall knowing that Talam was ill, but supposed he had forgotten. Ann Segrim looked crestfallen, and he took her hands in his by way of comforting her. They were soft and unlike any hand that Ralph had held recently. The voice of Brother John persisted like a bee buzzing in the Abbot's ear.

'Brother Peter has not been himself since the unfortunate death of the Bishop's brother. He seemed most upset by the incident. And his journey to Wallingford the other day did nothing to restore his health.'

'Wallingford? Did I know that he had gone to Wallingford?' Ralph was puzzled now. John Darby blushed at having apparently revealed something he should not have. Ann, on the other hand, was keen to hear more. Regent Master Falconer had asked her husband about a murder in Wallingford. Were her interests and his connected through her husband and Brother Talam? The prior was continuing to explain with some embarrassment.

'He . . . he went without your permission. For the best of reasons, I am sure. He wanted to offer spiritual support to the poor students who were involved in the killing. But I think he will deny it if confronted. He is so modest about his good acts, and in this case he is so despondent about his failure with the boy who killed himself. I am sorry for telling you – he swore me to secrecy after I had tried to dissuade him from going.'

Ralph patted Ann Segrim's hands.

'It would seem your journey has been fruitless. Unless Brother John or I can help? Although if it is to do with money matters, it would be best to speak with Brother Peter when he is . . . er . . . well again.'

He rose and Ann Segrim got up too, her robe draping elegantly on her full hips. The Abbot seemed disinclined to release Ann's hands, and reiterated his apology.

'Once again, I am sorry your time has been wasted.'

Ann smiled demurely, extricating her hands from the grip of the Abbot. She was more determined than ever now to see Falconer.

'Oh, it's not been entirely wasted. I have learned something useful.'

She turned to follow the prior who led her from the cloister, leaving Ralph to return to his dreams of an earlier time and an innocence that no longer existed. He completed the imaginary day from his youth with vespers.

If Guillaume de Beaujeu had sought out Brother Peter Talam that day, he might have been luckier than Ann Segrim. But having also seen the conspirators arriving at Botley from the cover of the walled garden, albeit on the other side from Falconer, he chose to seek out another of the people there. One he recognized without any difficulty. Aethelmar, Archbishop of Winchester, was well known to the Templars as a man with a secret. Indeed probably with many, but there was one that the Templars knew, and what his order knew in general was known by de Beaujeu in particular. Such was the way the order manipulated those in power to its own ends. The secret harked back long before Aethelmar was elevated to the bishopric, long before he and his Lusignan brothers came to England for the protection of their half-brother, the King.

De Beaujeu was patiently waiting in the ante-chamber to the Abbot's quarters in Abingdon. It had not been difficult to discover Aethelmar's presence from the network of spies the Templars employed across England. It had been a pleasant reward to find him so close to the abbey, and the continuing residence there of the Papal Legate made it doubly so. As the Legate had precedence over the Archbishop, the King's quarters were occupied by Bishop Otho, and Aethelmar had taken over the rooms belonging to the Abbot. That unfortunate old man had been relegated to the common dormitory with his monastic brethren.

The Templar had sent a message to the Archbishop which he knew would ensure the man's attention. Predictably, Aethelmar now emerged from the inner rooms, his face as white as a sheet. He bustled over to de Beaujeu and began to speak, though his tongue seemed to be stuck to the roof of his mouth. The Templar calmly put his finger to his lips, and nodded at the servant hovering behind the fat bishop. Waving away Boniface, who had been entrusted with delivering de Beaujeu's short message, Aethelmar stuttered a few words.

'What do you know of Mildred?'

De Beaujeu's face was impassive.

'And who are you?'

'Let us just say the Temple of Solomon is my home. And through that I know that Mildred is dead.'

There was a pause while Aethelmar's mind raced as he considered the choices open to him. Did the Templars know anything? Was this just a bluff?

The man spoke again, his voice cold and impersonal.

'And who killed her. And in what circumstances.'

Aethelmar began to bluster, but his pale face betrayed his concern.

'And why should that be any business of mine? Did I say I knew anyone called Mildred?'

'You have no need to say anything. But I shall say something, to convince you of the scope of my knowledge. Of course, I may have to say it also in the presence of your sister-in-law, or even the King, if this interview has an unsatisfactory result. The facts are these – Mildred was twelve years old, and when the body was buried, it was unclothed and showed . . .'

'Enough.'

Aethelmar shuddered, and his face was covered in sweat as though he were gripped by a fever. His stubby fingers rubbed at his jaw, down which spittle ran from his quivering lips.

'What is it you want, this satisfactory result?'

'Only an audience with the Papal Legate.'

Aethelmar gasped.

'I cannot do that. You would . . .'

He left the thought unspoken, and began another.

'I would be going against the King's express wishes, and if he were to find out . . .'

Once again, he could not find the strength to say what was on his mind. But he fingered his fat neck nervously, as though already feeling the stroke that would sever his head from his body. De Beaujeu was calm but relentless.

'How would he discover your complicity? Of course, if you preferred him to discover some other information . . .'

This time, de Beaujeu left his thought unspoken. But it was clear to the Archbishop what his choice was now, and he made it.

'It may take some time. To arrange the audience.'

'I can wait, but not too long.'

Chapter Ten

Falconer had hurried back from his morning lecture and sought the seclusion of his room. He needed to blend the involvement of the Chancellor-to-be into the plot he was imagining around the person of Humphrey Segrim. His mind was racing and he sought to suppress his flights of fancy with a controlled scientific exercise on another topic altogether.

He had got Hugh Pett to boil down the carcass of a chicken and supply him with all the bones. They now lay on the table in front of him in a bewildering jumble and he toyed with them absently. The faint aroma of chicken flesh still clung to them and Falconer's mouth watered, although he fancied his sense of smell was dulled. He hoped his involuntary immersion in the stream the other night was not going to result in a fever. Anyway, he thought, the meat had already made a good broth for the twenty students in Aristotle's Hall and was now but a memory. Falconer licked his fingers and began to concentrate on laying out the bones in the order they had occupied in the living bird.

He was impressed by their lightness compared to human bones and wondered again if he would ever understand the concept of flight so as to allow a man to fly. It was Roger Bacon who had encouraged him in this quest. Recalling the papers from his friend, he was about to turn to his storage chest where they lay when there came a thunderous knocking on the main door below. Cursing the disturbance of his thought processes, both on flight and on the murders, Falconer descended the creaking staircase to find out who was so anxious to see him.

Grumbling, he flung the heavy door open and before he could

react was grasped firmly by both arms. In front of him stood the grim figure of a soldier dressed in a bright red tunic that covered a shirt of light chain mail. Either side of him, expertly pinioning his arms, was a soldier similarly garbed. There seemed no point in struggling, so Falconer kept his temper.

'If you've come for tutelage, the lecture is over. You'll have to come back tomorrow morning. So if you don't mind, I'll bid you good-day.'

The man in charge was clearly not impressed by his humour and grunted his orders.

'You're to come with us.'

The other two pulled him firmly forward out of the doorway. Even Falconer's poor eyes could tell that the lane was strangely silent. And yet the sun was high, and the day only half gone. There should have been the normal bustle of passers-by. Indeed he could hear the distant shouts of traders and argumentative students coming from the High Street, which served only to make the silence close around him all the more eerie.

As he was hustled along under the walls of the city towards East Gate, he could see that there were strategically placed soldiers in red tunics at each end of the lane where Aristotle's stood. It was clear nobody was going to be allowed to interrupt his abduction. His heart pounded in his chest, and he was beginning to get worried. With no one to observe his disappearance, who could he hope would provide his salvation? Perhaps he should cry out when they reached the gates of the city. Someone must see him and report such an unusual incident. At the top of the lane, by the gates, stood another soldier with the reins of six horses in his hands. The man's face was dark-skinned and a huge grin split his leathery features, clearly indicating his pleasure that the little exercise had been accomplished successfully.

Falconer was no lightweight, but his captors hoisted him with apparent ease on to the back of one of the horses. He screwed round in the saddle to look for someone in the street to whom he could appeal. It seemed that every face was turned away from him, and he was confronted with the incongruous image of a cheerful, sunlit High Street filled with ordinary people going about their business as if nothing was amiss. And for them, nothing was. They were not being abducted by a group of silent and efficient soldiers, and carried off to an unknown fate. His horse was slapped on the rump by the grim-faced soldier and they careered under the arch of the gateway and out of Oxford.

Peter Bullock hurried away from the Golden Cross Inn, very anxious to speak to Falconer. He lumbered across the High Street, ignoring the stench from the open sewage channel in the middle and the cries of the shopkeepers alike. His mind was set on what he had discovered in the baggage of the mystery man who was dogging the Regent Master's footsteps. The sun was high in a clear blue sky and the familiar smells of the city were trapped by the stillness of the heat. Bullock should have felt comforted by the stink of humanity, draped around him like a cloak. The sweet smell of sweat on a working man reminded him of his days as a soldier, toiling side by side with men who depended on each other to survive. Even, God save him, the acrid smell of piss spoke to him of camps and comradeship.

But now these everyday smells did not enter his thoughts. His mind was churning over the items he had unearthed at the Golden Cross. It had been simple to gain access to the man's room, even though the landlord had been unusually frightened. Apparently the man had insisted on a room that could be locked, and had kept what he thought was the only key. Bullock knew any landlord worth his salt had a spare key, and a threat no longer to turn a blind eye to watered-down beer had persuaded this landlord to allow Bullock in. And the threat of revealing the landlord's duplicity would ensure he kept his mouth shut when the stranger returned.

At first there had seemed very little to see. A straw-filled mattress lay atop the low wooden bunk, and the remains of a simple meal were stacked neatly on the rickety table. A plain chair was the only other ornament to the otherwise empty chamber. No doubt there were plenty of cockroaches to keep the man company at night, but there was little to betray his purpose.

In the farthest corner lay a leather satchel of the sort that could be slung over the haunches of a horse. Bullock decided to see what it contained. But first he shut the door on the anxious face of the Golden Cross's landlord. Crossing the room, he was reminded of his own days as a man-at-arms. The neatness of the stacked pots and the lack of clothes that you might expect to find scattered around the room, suggested to him a man ready to move at a moment's notice. Or at a clarion call to arms. With interest he sat on the end of the bed and hefted the large and supple satchel on to his knees. He untied the cords that held the flap down and poked his hand inside. At first it was disappointing. There was merely a change of clothes – some leggings and a neat but anonymous tunic. He placed them carefully on the bed, folded as they had been in the bag. The stranger was so tidy, he would inevitably notice if his baggage had been riffled by someone else. Beneath was a garment of more interest – a suit of light chain mail. This confirmed for Bullock that he was dealing with someone with a noble background and battle experience. In his day a heavy banded mail coat of links of iron sewn on to leather had been common. It had been awkward and restricting in battle. More recently, the lighter interlinked chain mail had found favour with the true warrior. Someone at the centre of a battle needed freedom of action, not like those courtly knights who sat at the back of skirmishes like stuffed dummies with as much mobility as a Norman tower.

He thought he had gleaned all he safely could, and he was carefully restoring the clothes to their original position when his clumsy fingers snagged in what he at first surmised was a split in the seam of the leather. Except underneath his fingers he could hear the crackle of parchment or paper.

* * *

Ann Segrim impatiently fingered the gold ornaments she was offered by the smith. After her conversation with Ralph Harbottle at Oseney Abbey, she was more anxious than ever to find William Falconer and talk to him. What she had inadvertently learned about the monk, Brother Talam, and his trip to Wallingford could be vital to his investigations. And to her seeking the truth about her husband's activities. However, she had her servant, Sekston, in tow and could not be sure that he would not report any meeting back to her husband. She would have to get rid of him somehow.

First she had to go through the pretence of selecting some jewellery, which had been her original pretext for visiting Oxford. The goldsmith was an obsequious but persistent man, who kept thrusting something else at her every time she considered but declined one of his offerings. She did like his work but did not want to buy – nor could she afford it, if the truth were known.

At last she managed to convince him that there was nothing she wanted, and returned his final piece, a rather nice gold brooch of modern design. The man looked downcast as she left the shop and walked down the main street dogged by urchins. Her servant followed close behind and cuffed the urchins away with a series of swift blows to their lice-ridden heads. She walked nearly to East Gate before she turned abruptly and, with the demeanour of an indecisive wife, thrust some coins at Sekston.

'I really want that brooch after all. Go and see if he will reduce his price for me.'

Sekston protested that he could not leave her alone, but Ann stifled his objections with an imperious look. He shrugged and did as he was told. Perhaps she did have an assignation with a lover. If so, she wasn't about to tell of his dereliction of duty, and he might even have time to enjoy a few ales before returning. She certainly looked keen to be rid of him. He just wondered who the lucky man was.

As Sekston's back disappeared in the crowd, Ann looked for someone who might be able to help her find the Regent Master.

Seeing someone dressed in the same garb as Falconer across the street, she resolved to ask him where the latter lived. How likely it was he knew the man she sought, she did not know, but then she had to make a start. The soberly clad man was deep in conversation with a baker outside his shop. Crossing the street, she heard the end of the conversation, which turned out to be an argument over the price of a loaf. The Master turned away in disgust, clearly not prepared to pay the asking price, and almost bumped into Ann.

He offered his confused apologies, then smiled wryly when asked if perchance he knew of Master Falconer.

'Who does not?'

His smiling face did not offer any more information, so Ann was forced to ask if he also knew where Falconer lived. As if it were some game of pedantry with one of his students, the man merely nodded. Impatient but not showing it, Ann was ultimately forced to ask where his residence was located. Apparently satisfied that she had framed her question in the appropriate manner, he finally pointed Ann to the nearby alley down which she needed to go to find Aristotle's Hall. She thanked him courteously, though it was more than he deserved. She left him thinking enviously of Falconer's luck in attracting such a beautiful woman, and recalling the softness of the bosom he had bumped against.

Hurrying down the narrow alley, she started to have second thoughts about her actions. She began to wonder how she would approach Falconer, who might not even remember her from their chance encounter in the walled garden. After all, she had not spoken to him then. The alley was gloomy now, as light could only penetrate between the closely packed houses in the middle of the day. The sun was well past its zenith, and Ann shivered. The man had told her that Aristotle's Hall stood between two lanes running across her path towards East Gate. After crossing the first lane, she came to a dark doorway facing east. She assumed this must be it.

Strangely, the door was ajar and there was no sound from within. She hesitated, not knowing whether to proceed, and called out nervously. There was no response, and steeling her resolve she stepped over the threshold. She was in a large hall at the centre of which stood a heavy, scarred trestle table. It was obviously the survivor of many a carefree repast enjoyed by boisterous students. The top was stained with carelessly spilled ale and wine. Initials had been carved on the surface and smoothed with time. It was redolent of cheerful camaraderie. But the hall was strangely silent.

She called Falconer's name but there was no reply. Then, standing in the midst of the quiet, she thought she heard a returning call from up above. She moved to the rickety wooden staircase that leaned precariously against the side wall close to the door where she had come in. Lifting her by now dusty skirts above the crackling rushes on the floor, she nervously climbed the stairs, step by step.

At the top she stopped again, hearing a muffled call from the door nearest to her. It was slightly ajar, and she could see a beam of sunlight illuminating the room beyond.

'Master Falconer, are you there?'

Her voice trembled, but this time there was no response. Uncertain, she pushed the door open. The room revealed was a jumble of jars, books and bones – the very lair of a necromancer. But with the door swung wide, it was clearly empty. She stepped across the threshold, enticed by the mixture of sights and smells in the room. She bent to examine the book that lay open on the table, as if it might give some clue to Falconer's whereabouts – and shrieked as a white apparition swooped from the darkest corner and became entangled in her hair. She ducked, blindly swinging her arms above her head in panic. She thought the very Devil had hold of her and she was fighting for her life.

Mercifully she was released as swiftly as she had been taken, and the apparition returned to its corner. She felt her legs give way, and sat down hard on the rough wooden floor. After a few moments, she summoned the courage to look up, and burst out laughing. High on a pole, above a wall splashed with white stains, a barn owl perched preening its ruffled feathers. At her laughter it looked down at her with such solemn eyes that it caused a renewed fit of giggles. With difficulty she gained control and apologized to the bird.

'Forgive me, Sir Owl, if I laughed at you. You are quite the most handsome gentleman I've seen, and I am sorry if I mistook you for the Devil. I don't suppose you know where your master is, do you?'

At first she thought the bird had responded when a voice spoke.

'I would like to know where he is, too.'

Then she realized the voice had come from the doorway, and turned her head to see who it was who also sought the Regent Master. She recognized the burly, hunch-backed frame of the custodian of law in Oxford, and breathed a sigh of relief. Then she remembered she was still sitting on the floor, and blushed to match the colour of her dress. Bullock stepped forward and offered her his hand. She accepted it, and felt the power of his callused grip as she recovered a more seemly position on her feet.

They stood facing each other and there was an awkward silence. Oddly, he appeared to be embarrassed at being found out in Falconer's room by her, rather than the other way round. Ann Segrim spoke first.

'I came to see Master Falconer, but he appears not to be at home.'

'So it seems. You should not have left the door open behind you, you know. I am afraid there are too many thieves in the town.'

Ann sought to excuse herself.

'Oh, but it was already open, or I would not have come in.'

Bullock frowned.

'Left open? That is unlike Master Falconer. Still, perhaps it was one of his careless students. I shall have to speak to him when he returns.'

After another pause, when there seemed little else to say, he turned to leave. Ann followed him down the creaking stairs, disappointed at having missed the Master. At the front door she waited as Bullock closed it firmly behind him.

'Will you tell Master Falconer that I have some information that may interest him?'

'When I next see him I will pass on your message, Mistress Segrim.'

Their conversation was strained, and she thanked him and hurried back up the narrow alley to the High Street. So she missed his gloomy, muttered aside.

'If I ever see him again.'

The object of Bullock's concern was equally worried about his fate. At that very moment he sat on a rough-hewn bench in a bare room that was both dark and cold. It resembled the crypt of a church, with a low stone ceiling that was prevented from bearing down on him by a row of squat pillars arching over his head. A dusty beam of late afternoon light filtered weakly down on him from a narrow slit high in the end arch. The floor was merely packed earth, and was covered with the tracks of scurrying creatures that he felt sure still prowled in the darker recesses of the room. His mood was once again plummeting to the lower depths where he imagined the rats might lurk. Whose hand was behind this, and how far would they go? Would de Cantilupe have acted in this way? Did Segrim think he had uncovered too many secrets to remain alive? None of the soldiers who had brought him here would utter a word to explain who they were acting for.

After snatching him and leaving Oxford through East Gate, the troop had swung round to the south side of the town and had galloped hard towards Wallingford. As Falconer clung on to his swiftly moving mount, he thought of the hapless end John Gryffin had met in the dungeon of the castle there. The reins of his horse were held firmly on either side by two of the stony-faced soldiers. The shanks of their mounts pressed his legs uncomfortably against his horse. He was in effect pinioned on a horse he could not rein in, riding to God knows where, surrounded by determined men who did not care to say what was going to happen to him.

The dust from the road, now dried to a hard pan by days of unusually fine weather, rose in a cloud around the closely packed group of riders. It caught in Falconer's throat, already dry with fear of what was surely to come. He hawked and spat a gobbet of brown dust and phlegm, turning in his saddle to avoid his captors. His aim was poor and the projectile splattered on the clean red surcoat of the soldier on his right. The man seemed unaware as the gobbet slid down, defiling his uniform. Falconer's spirits rose a little at that point.

Not many miles outside Oxford the tight phalanx had wheeled to the right and forded the river with hardly a pause in the horses' stride. The soldiers then followed an unfamiliar track through a heavily wooded landscape. Trees overhung the route, and despite the dry weather the horses had to plough through muddy pools that were splashed up by the flashing hooves. Several times Falconer bent low, along with his captors, to avoid branches that threatened to pluck the riders from their mounts. Despite that, there was no reining back on the speed of their progress.

Eventually they broke out of the woods and thundered down a well-worn track to an imposing group of buildings, dominated by a church and cloisters, on the edge of a substantial settlement. The sun was low and in Falconer's eyes, but the buildings looked familiar. As he was pulled from his mount and bundled through the main courtyard, he suddenly realized he was at the King's hall in the abbey at Abingdon. He had been disorientated by arriving from a different direction than normal, avoiding Nuneham and the main highway. Clearly his captor did not want anyone to know he was here.

* * *

Bullock watched the woman disappear up the lane, and re-entered Aristotle's Hall. He was convinced there was something amiss. Falconer simply would not have left his front door ajar, and none of his young charges was careless enough to do so. He dragged himself back up to Falconer's room and scanned it closely. To the unfamiliar eye, there would have been no difference between how it appeared now and its normal state of disorder. But the scattered bird bones on the table spoke to Peter Bullock of Falconer being interrupted in the midst of his studies. And not being able to return to them. He knew the Regent Master was fanatical about concluding a line of thought, once begun. After all, this trait had often irritated him when they were both engaged on a murder investigation. No, he would not have left the little puzzle of bones incomplete unless he had been forcibly removed.

'What do you think, Balthazar?'

He looked at the barn owl, who merely returned his quizzical stare.

'Did you see what happened?'

Balthazar's unblinking eyes gave Bullock no crumb of comfort. Then, oblivious to Bullock's concern, the owl responded to imperatives of his own. He hopped over to the open window arch, launched himself through it, and gracefully flew off to his hunting grounds. He left the constable fingering the document he had purloined from the Frenchman's saddlebag, and wishing Falconer were around to advise him.

The Regent Master was feeling hungry. He seemed to have been forgotten in his private dungeon, and the passage of the feeble ray of light across the dusty floor marked out the length of time he had been ignored. He knew his young students would shortly be returning to the hall for their supper. And meagre though it might be, he longed for what they would now be eating. Thoughts of the stalest bread and flattest ale caused his digestive juices to gurgle in his stomach. Even Balthazar would be on the wing, to begin his silent search for food. How he envied the bird's ability to escape the confinement of four walls. He looked up wistfully at the narrow slit of a window, far beyond his reach. To compound his difficulties, his head was thumping and his throat felt as though it was lined with feathers. Friar Fordam might not have killed him, but by causing him to bathe fully clothed he had ensured the onset of a fever. He cursed his ill-luck, and imagined himself as a Christian martyr entombed until Judgement Day.

The screeching sound of a bolt being withdrawn alerted him once again to the possibility of further bad fortune. He stepped back from the door as it swung open and adopted a wrestler's stance, his body balanced and ready. He would fight for his life if need be.

The Sixth Seal

Also in the year 1250, there were earthquakes in the Chilterns on St Lucy's Day. This has never been reported before by those who live in Ciltria. Accompanying the movement was a terrifying noise akin to thunder under the ground. Jackdaws, pigeons and sparrows took to wing and flew to and fro in confusion, as though they were hunted by a sparrowhawk. The new moon appeared both swollen and reddish in the sky. Then was the Sixth Seal broken. And it is written that there was a violent earthquake, and the moon turned red as blood. All men, rich or poor, monarch or slave, hid themselves in caves to conceal them from the Lord. It is at this time that the seal of our God will be set upon the forehead of the tribes of the new Israel to denote those who will be saved. I await the breaking of the Seventh Seal.

From the *Chronica Oseneiensis*

Chapter Eleven

'I apologize, Master Falconer, for the inconvenience, but it was for your own safety, I assure you.'

In the doorway stood Humphrey Segrim, a self-satisfied smile on his flushed face. He clearly wished to disarm Falconer by his statement, but a burly, red-coated soldier stood close at his shoulder nevertheless. Segrim stepped fastidiously into the cell, wishing to avoid sullying his soft leather boots on the dusty, dropping-covered floor. He linked his arm with Falconer's, feeling the tension in the Master's frame.

'I have something to show you.'

Falconer allowed himself to be led out of the cell and up the stone staircase which, descending, he had not expected to see again. This time he was drawn in the opposite direction by Segrim, into a lavishly appointed passageway lined with tapestries. Torches lit the way with splashes of light. Passing a glazed window, Falconer saw that evening had fallen and all he could see was the pale reflection of his own face. He suddenly realized that Segrim had been speaking to him.

'I'm sorry, what did you say?'

'I was saying that what you are about to witness should convince you that it is nonsensical to pursue any feud against me or my colleagues.'

'Feud?'

'In the matter of the unfortunate death of Sinibaldo. The Papal Legate's brother.'

Falconer caught Segrim's arm firmly and stopped him in his tracks. There was a flash of alarm in Segrim's eyes, and he looked over Falconer's shoulder at the man-at-arms who was still in attendance. The man took a step towards Falconer, his hand on a dagger at his waist. Falconer visibly relaxed, patted Segrim's arm and smiled at the soldier. He spoke in lowered tones.

'Don't you think it would be better to discuss all this in private, without other ears hearing what we say? Anyway you don't need your nursemaid so close. It would be foolish of me to seek to harm you, with so many soldiers around.'

Segrim thought a moment, then nodded, and motioned for the soldier to leave them.

When the man had retreated out of sight, Falconer turned back to Segrim. For the first time that evening he discerned a thin film of sweat on the man's florid face, despite the coldness of the corridor they stood in. He was also picking at the sleeve of his richly decorated robe, pulling golden threads loose from the embroidery. It was more than mere nervousness at Falconer's physical presence. There was something important afoot that he was seeking to do, and he was more than a little worried about failing. Falconer continued the interrupted conversation, his curiosity aroused.

'What makes you think I am conducting a feud against you?'

Segrim regained a little of his composure.

'Because you are spreading ridiculous rumours that I was involved in the death of Sinibaldo. That somehow I had arranged to kill Bishop Otho on behalf of the King, and bungled it.'

Segrim cackled at this statement, as though the very idea was ridiculous. To Falconer's ears, the laughter sounded hollow. He thought he might try to provoke the man into further revelations.

'I am not spreading any rumour. I am merely collecting the facts and trying to deduce a greater truth from them. Why should I not consider the possibility that you did try to arrange the death of the Bishop?'

Segrim's jowls shook as he tried to control himself, and his normally soft features tightened, his lips white and drawn. He spoke not a word, but took Falconer's arm again and led him on down the passageway. Once more in control of himself, he chose his words carefully.

'I see I cannot convince you. That like Doubting Thomas you must see for yourself. Then so be it, you will see.'

He almost dragged the mystified Falconer to the foot of a spiral staircase, where he stopped and thrust his face at the Master.

'I must insist, however, that you are perfectly silent from now on,' he hissed.

Leading the way, Segrim crept up the staircase and Falconer followed, trying not to cause the wooden steps to creak under his weight. At the top Segrim beckoned Falconer forward with an urgent wave of his arm. The Regent Master saw they were in what must be a minstrels' gallery. The narrow balcony had solid timber panelling to waist height, and above that a row of artfully carved posts that afforded a restricted view down into the hall below. From the main hall, the musicians would be invisible to the assembled throng of nobles, their music apparently drifting down from heaven. On this occasion, both Segrim and Falconer were hidden from whoever was below, and could spy on them without being seen.

Falconer could hear a murmur of voices, and it was clear the hall was well lit by the glow that filtered through the lattice-work. The gallery was hot and stuffy from the many torches that illuminated the scene below. Segrim motioned for the Regent Master to move forward, but as Falconer opened his mouth to form a question he quickly put his finger to his lips. Falconer obeyed and moved to the screen, hoping a sneeze from his blocked-up nose would not betray his presence.

He peered between the carving and cursed his poor eyesight. But screwing up his eyes, he could just make out the scene down in the hall. Bright tapestries hung from the walls, the extravagant creatures on them apparently alive as the light flickered on their surfaces. Unicorn jousted with lion in a mythical battle of the beasts, whilst in the next panel allegorical figures lived out ancient tales. Beneath this other-worldly opulence, the small group of men seemed almost insignificant. They had clearly finished a lavish meal, the remnants of which lay thrust aside on trestle tables. Trenchers were crumbled and broken, and stains of wine and gravy mingled across the tables' surfaces. The men now sat round the hearth in the centre of the vast hall, the flames of the fire lighting up their faces.

Falconer squinted at the pinkish blobs that should hold some significance, if Segrim's clandestine exercise were to be taken seriously. He studied them as hard as his weakened eyesight would allow. Most of the group were facing towards him, looking at the man whose back was firmly set to Falconer's view. This man was grey haired and of moderate stature, his body compact, but even seated he had a naturally noble bearing. The others seemed to hang on his every word, but his voice was low and Falconer could not make out what he was saying. He looked back at Segrim in frustration. What was this supposed to tell him?

Peter Talam waited until after vespers, when all of his fellow monks had retired to the dorter or to their separate cells. Dusk was settling over the water-meadows surrounding Oseney Abbey, and it was time for him to move. In the uncertain light, it became difficult to tell a man from the scrubby trees that littered the meadows, if the man stood quite still. Anyway, there was little likelihood of there being anyone to observe him at this hour. The countryside outside the walls of Oxford fell silent after the sun had gone down.

The monk felt in his purse for the little vial that contained the potion he had so carefully prepared that day in his solitary cell. The comforting shape was still there, and he patted it gently and smiled. If the properties of the brew were to be believed, this would sort matters out once and for all. He slipped out of the small door cut in the face of the massive doors that secured the abbey for the night. His route through the darkened landscape was familiar to him, which was just as well as the light was fast disappearing. Hanging low over the trees ahead of him, the rising moon looked red and ominous, and he shivered, pulling his robes around him for protection. He uttered a brief prayer and scurried down the dusty track, as a distant rumble of thunder warned of a storm.

High in the Scriptorium, where he had gone to retrieve a valuable text he had not intended to leave out overnight, Brother John Darby shielded the guttering candle from reflecting on the window, and looked out. He had thought he had seen something moving in the courtyard, but assumed his own reflection in the glass had deceived him. Now, on a more careful look, he saw a monk stepping through the wicket door and closing it behind him. He was sure from the way the monk moved, stiffly and upright, that it had been Peter Talam. He wondered where the bursar was going when the rules demanded that he be a-bed, and pondered on telling the Abbot. Whatever he was about, it must be of some secrecy.

Falconer was growing exasperated with the lack of action, as he sat looking down on the lengthy conversation of this group of people whom he could not even identify. He squirmed in his hard and uncomfortable seat, but Segrim merely smiled secretively and raised his palm to indicate Falconer should be patient. At that moment the door at the end of the hall was flung open and all the heads turned away from the grey-haired man in expectation. A thin, clerkish figure appeared in the archway, clinging to the heavy door. It looked as though the door had swung open of its own volition with this scrawny figure hanging on to it, rather than having been moved in its frame by the insignificant clerk. Clearly this was not the man everyone in the chamber was anticipating, for the group below Falconer still waited eagerly for the new arrival.

A thick and heavily accented voice boomed out from beyond the doorway.

'Your Majesty, thank you for agreeing to see me again.'

The archway was filled with the gaudily clad and corpulent shape of Bishop Otho, the Papal Legate to England. Falconer recognized him instantly despite the distance and his poor eyesight. There could be no other man in England who was so obviously – well – Roman. Only after he had identified the new player in the tableau below did the import of the Bishop's words register on Falconer's brain. Otho had referred to 'Your Majesty'. The grey-haired man of upright bearing was King Henry III of England.

Bishop Otho waddled towards the King, his arms held forward in an open gesture of Mediterranean warmth. Light flashed off the many rings on his stubby fingers. Henry stood his ground and, despite his moderate physical stature, caused the Bishop to turn his intended hug into a grasping of the King's outstretched hand. The Bishop also converted his forward lunge into a hasty and wobbly genuflection, and the men's relative positions of power were established.

However, with this tacitly agreed, Henry put his arm round the bulky shoulders of the Bishop, lifting him up and treating him as a friend. He guided the cleric towards a large and comfortable chair set next to his own. In doing so, he turned his face towards Falconer for the first time. By squinting, the Regent Master could make out a thin, pale face set in a worried frown, creases lining his high forehead. The grey thatch of hair plunging in waves either side of the drawn cheeks was matched by a grey beard that was carefully combed to a point. The face certainly resembled a likeness of the King, executed by Brother Darby, that Falconer had been shown in the Oseney Abbey chronicles. He glanced at the shadowy figure of Humphrey Segrim by his side. The man looked smug.

He clearly relished the opportunity to show others the high circles with which he consorted.

For Falconer, returning his gaze to the scene below was like looking at one of the mythical tableaux on the wall tapestries. There sat the King of England in discourse with the Papal Legate, surrounded by what must be some of the most influential nobles in England. The conversation was at first too low for Falconer to hear, as the two powerful men leaned close to each other. Then the King asked a question of one of the men surrounding him, there was laughter and the talking continued at a level audible to Falconer.

'My Lord Bishop, I can assure you that all goes well now.'

The King's voice was thin and reedy, but carried a note of confidence that suggested he was amongst people he trusted. No one here would question his authority, as de Montfort and some other barons were doing. No one here would question his surrounding himself with foreign advisers. Some present, no doubt, were Savoyard or Roman.

'The money is now accruing from the abbeys and monasteries. I told you to have patience and all would fall into place.'

The Bishop inclined his head, bowing to the King's better judgement.

'Your subjects are most generous.'

The other men in the group found this uproariously funny, but the King quietened their unruly behaviour with an upraised hand. Otho clearly did not understand what he had said to cause the laughter, and gazed at Henry with a puzzled look on his florid features. The King carried on as though nothing had happened.

'We should soon have enough funds to enable our proper support of your candidacy to replace Pope Alexander. We can ensure that the church is illumined by your guidance, and a pious peace will prevail to our mutual advantage.'

Falconer's racing brain could hardly take in the import of what was being said. But down below, the bulky frame of the Bishop seemed to puff up even more from the flattery of the English King. He flung himself from his chair and planted a kiss on each cheek of the startled monarch.

'And in return I will reinstate your family's right to the throne of Sicily, and . . .'

The King hurriedly put a ringed finger to his lips and cut off the flow of promises from the Bishop. In response Otho gave a grotesquely knowing wink, but could not curtail his excitement. A voluble flow of words in his own tongue was cast in the direction of his secretary, the thin functionary who had preceded his entrance. Stepping from the shadows, the man paled at what was clearly a set of extravagant promises, but nodded to denote he had consigned them to his memory. The Bishop whispered eagerly into the ear of the King, no doubt translating his promises into the English tongue. But even this was eventually waved aside by Henry, and the Bishop bowed obsequiously. He then backed out of the hall, pausing only to throw several extravagant obeisances at the King, his robes twirling around his gesticulating hands.

As the door closed behind him with a crash that echoed up the hall, Falconer felt Segrim's hand on his shoulder.

'You've seen enough,' he hissed.

The Regent Master was reluctant to take his gaze off the scene below, but the conversation had now been lowered once again to conspiratorial tones. He had indeed seen and heard enough. There was obviously a compact between King Henry and the Bishop. In return for the King's moral and monetary support in his quest for the papal throne, the Bishop was to offer the titbit of an entire kingdom and more. There was clearly no reason why the King, or any of his supporters including Segrim, would be involved in plotting the Bishop's death. Falconer's edifice of truths was rapidly crumbling, and even though his thought processes were dulled by his chill, he knew he had been in error. The confident look on Segrim's face meant he knew Falconer had reached the right conclusion.

Chapter Twelve

The pale yellow dawn cast a feeble ray into the Regent Master's room, almost too weak to push away the gloom. The darkness of the chamber seemed to gain its strength from the figure hunched over the heavy oaken table. His muscular shoulders twitched involuntarily and a powerful sneeze stirred him to wakefulness. Bleary-eyed, he scanned the room vacantly, his head ringing with the aftershock of the sneeze. Bad enough that he could no longer see a way forward to discovering the true identity of Sinibaldo's murderer. Now he was being laid low with a fever. His head felt stuffed with old rags, and all his limbs ached unmercifully. He breathed in the chill air of the room, and his chest popped and rattled like some ill-fitted water-wheel.

Trying to rise, he felt dizzy and slumped back on to the bench, resting his aching head on his folded arms. He tried to think clearly and sneezed again. It had all been so lucid at the start of the previous day. Segrim, or a monkish accomplice, had arranged for the Welshman to fire an arrow at the Bishop during a concocted riot. They had then sought out the unfortunate youth and ensured his silence by strangling him. It mattered not that John Gryffin had killed the wrong man. Indeed that had been all the more reason to punish his failure with death.

He had worried a little over the strange position of the body in the kitchen, and moreover there was the recent gouge in the wooden pillar. What had caused that, and was it important? He had wished he could speak to the servants who had been present to tidy up these loose ends in his imagined tapestry. He shook his befuddled brain. Yesterday he had cast aside these minor facts.

After all, not everything could always be fitted into place. Now, it seemed nothing fitted. If Segrim had no reason to kill the Bishop, in fact had every reason to protect him, the truths he had collected did not match at all. As if reflecting the state of Falconer's thinking, the early morning sun was obscured by cloud, and a depressing greyness fell across the room.

Guillaume de Beaujeu was angry. He had still not heard from that fat, murdering Archbishop about getting access to Otho. What's more, he had wasted a good night's sleep, keeping an eye on Aethelmar's co-conspirator. He had returned in the early hours of the morning to his room at the Golden Cross Inn after a chilly night observing the comings and goings at Oseney Abbey. The dank and penetrating vapours of the low-lying marshy land had bitten deep into his bones. He had even found himself wishing once more for the sharp but sere cold of the desert nights in the Holy Land. His vigil had been doubly uncomfortable because he could smell the aroma of the meal the monks had eaten earlier, and could sense the warmth spilling out into the night from the dorter wing where self-indulgent monks had candles burning yellowly long after the sun had set. The heat had not reached him, squeezed as he was behind the low scrub that lined a foetid drainage channel. In the end no one had ventured beyond the walls of the abbey. Or so he assumed – much to his mortification, he realized in the middle of the night that he had dozed off. Waking with a red moon hanging low in the sky, he did not know whether he had slept for a moment or a long time. He scanned the water-meadows for movement but there was none, and everything seemed as it had before his eyes had closed.

Now he had returned to his room to find his saddle panniers disturbed. Whoever had examined them had taken care to replace them in the same position in an attempt to hide his actions. But de Beaujeu knew the knot on the cord that held the flap down was not his. He fingered it thoughtfully, then untied the unfamiliar knot and opened the bags. His few possessions were still inside, so the intruder had not been a common thief. His hand then went automatically to the secret compartment, sliding his fingers into the supple leather. With a start he realized the letter had gone.

He let out a curse in his own tongue and called angrily for the landlord of the inn. The man was at his door in an instant, betraying the fact that he must have been hovering nearby, nervous of the Frenchman's return. He was doubly betrayed by the petrified look on his face that an obsequious smile failed to mask. De Beaujeu strode over and grasped a handful of the landlord's stained and coarse shirt. He twisted the cloth tight around the other's neck and slammed him against the inner wall of his room. The cheap daub cracked and a chunk fell loose at their feet.

The red-faced landlord squawked and scrabbled with roughened fingers at the Frenchman's steely grip. De Beaujeu shot just one word at him.

'Who?'

Seeing a reluctance in the man's eyes to respond to his question, he grasped a knot of his greasy hair and cracked his head sharply against the crumbling wall. The landlord's eyes squeezed tight with pain, and the words poured out of his mouth.

'It was Bullock, the constable. He made me do it.'

De Beaujeu loosened his grip and strode out of the inn, leaving the landlord to slide down the broken wall into a quivering heap.

'Thank God you are safe.'

Peter Bullock stood in the doorway of William Falconer's room, a nervous Hugh Pett peering from behind his crooked shoulders.

'Your young student let me in. I had been hammering at the hall door for an age. It was a good job he and the others were returning from their morning lectures. Why didn't you answer?'

He paused in his volley of anxious questions and peered more closely at his friend. 'You look awful.'

Falconer groaned and whispered through a hoarse throat.

'What time is it?'

'It's near to sext. The middle of the day and you haven't yet stirred. You must be ill.'

Falconer rose groggily, wiped his dripping nose on the sleeve of his robe and closed the door in the startled face of young Pett. He turned to Bullock, who seemed to fill the room with his misshapen body.

'I'm fine. A little cold is all. And a heavy dose of disappointment.'

He beckoned Bullock to sit down and slumped on the bench beside him. An account of the events of the previous day followed, culminating with the revelation that he was entirely lost concerning the murders. Bullock, whose eyes had widened at the mention of King Henry, now leaned forward with a story of his own to tell. He told Falconer of his sightings of the mysterious man, how he followed him to the Golden Cross Inn and got the landlord to let him into the man's room. Falconer was mildly interested, but his sore eyes kept drooping and each wheezing breath was an effort. He just wished the constable would get his story over with and leave him to suffer in peace.

'And then I found this letter.'

Falconer looked up and saw that Bullock was triumphantly brandishing a folded piece of parchment, with a broken red wax seal on its outer surface.

'Who's it from?'

'You haven't been listening to a word, have you.'

Bullock's craggy features were crestfallen and Falconer regretted his inattention. The constable obviously thought he had something important, and the least he could do was appear interested – for the sake of their long friendship, if nothing else.

'Yes, I have. The mystery man is a warrior, you say. And what does the letter from his luggage prove?'

Once again a frown creased the already lined face of Peter Bullock.

'I was hoping you'd tell me. It's in a foreign language.'

He passed the folded letter to Falconer, and the two halves of the broken seal were united before the Regent Master's eyes. Suddenly, his curiosity was aroused, and he thought for the first time that Bullock might indeed have something interesting. He brought the red wax close to his face and followed the lines of the impressed shape with his fingers.

'What is it?' came the anxious voice of Peter Bullock.

'This is the crest of the Poor Knights of Christ and the Temple of Solomon. Templars, to you and me.'

Bullock beamed with pleasure that he had found something to attract Falconer's attention after all.

'What does the letter say?'

Falconer opened the stiffened sheet and scanned the letter quickly.

'It's in the French tongue. But I can read it.'

He read in silence, and Bullock shuffled uneasily on the bench, staring intently at his friend as though he could decipher the contents from Falconer's face.

'It's about a shipment of pottery from Northern France with a lot of details about the price of transportation, the route and the contents of the crates.'

Bullock was struck dumb. It was not at all what he expected – such a disappointment after waiting since yesterday, thinking this letter would solve all the mysteries of the master cook's death. Strangely, Falconer did not seem at all disappointed. With a quiet smile on his face, he swung round to face the table and spat on the dried remains of yesterday's ink. Mixing it together with a little water from the bottom of the jug that had been delivered for his ablutions, Falconer lifted up a quill and checked the quality of the point. Satisfied, he looked at the disconsolate Bullock.

'Don't you think it odd, my friend, that your warrior should be carrying a business document? And in a secret compartment too?'

'Well, perhaps, but . . .'

Falconer did not let him finish, and Bullock could tell that, despite his fever, his friend was in a familiar mood. He always became impish when he saw the solution to a puzzle no one else had spotted. The constable knew he would have to be patient and allow Falconer to tell it in his own way.

'You see, the Templars have fingers in many pies. Financial and political. In areas where information is very sensitive, and needs to be kept secret.'

Bullock nodded but could not see where this was leading, and why Falconer needed quill and ink. The Master continued.

'They often send messages within messages, and this letter is too innocuous on the surface to warrant being hidden. Therefore, there must be a hidden message in it.'

Bullock's disappointment was beginning to dissipate. A hidden message meant something important.

'But that gets us nowhere. How can we decipher it?'

'I happen to know some of their codes. Don't ask me why for it's a long story. But the commonest code is to scatter the true message using the second letter of the third word in each sentence. See how short these sentences are, and how long the text? Not normal for a simple business letter. It suggests to me there is a message hidden using that code. Whoever did it was very lazy to use such a common one, but that is our luck and the Templar's misfortune.'

He passed the letter to Bullock.

'You call out the letters and I'll write them down.'

Very soon a string of letters was scratched on a scrap of paper by Falconer's elderly quill.

A–U–N–O–M–D.

Bullock peered at the sequence and tried to mouth a word. He was disappointed.

'It's meaningless.'

'Have patience,' urged Falconer, and raised his quill to continue the task. Bullock counted and called out another sequence.

U–G–R–A–N–D–M.

Falconer felt a shiver up his spine, and was sure it was not the fever that caused it. The following letters confirmed his suspicion.

A–I–T–R–E.

He quickly scored lines after the second, fifth, seventh and twelfth letters on the paper.

'*"Au nom du Grand Maître"*. It's a letter from the Grand Master of the order himself, written in French. Carry on.'

The owner of the letter was frustrated in his search for the town constable. He was quite prepared to confront the man over his theft, and claim his letter back. It was, after all, an important business document. He was confident that Bullock would not be able to decipher the message containing the secret authorization of the Grand Master, and therefore he would be seen as an innocent wronged.

He knew from his earlier surveillance that the man lived below the Great Keep. But when he entered the gloomy courtyard he could see the door to the constable's quarters was firmly shut. There was no response to the insistent sound of his fist on the studded door. He quartered the city, expecting to run across Bullock patrolling the narrow lanes, again without success. The streets were full of rowdy students baiting each other, threatening to make the dusty alleys a battleground between those from the northern nation and those from the south. But of the constable there was no sign. His last resort was the home of the nosy Regent Master, William Falconer. He and Bullock were a strange pair, but obviously close friends. Loosening his sword in its scabbard, he retraced his steps towards East Gate and the narrow lane that led to Aristotle's Hall.

Gradually the letters hidden within the innocuous-seeming business document spelled out an authorization for the bearer from the Grand Master of the Templars. It was addressed to the supporter of the Orsini faction in the household of Bishop Otho. Tantalizingly, the name of this person was not mentioned in the body of the text they had deciphered so far. However, the last paragraph of the business letter began to reveal the instructions the bearer of the document had been commanded to follow. They were to do with the elimination of the Papal Legate, and demanded the cooperation of the Orsini agent. Bullock still did not understand what the import of the hidden message was.

'What's this Orsini?' he asked, pronouncing the middle syllable as 'sin'. Falconer corrected him, putting a long 'i' in the middle.

'The Orsini are a who, not a what. A very influential family indeed – cardinals, or wealthy supporters of cardinals.'

Falconer could already begin to see what was afoot.

'This is all about the politics of power in Rome itself. And the election of the next Pope. Let's finish the deciphering. There has to be a name somewhere for this agent.'

Eventually they found it. Bullock called out the letters and Falconer was ahead of him.

S–I–N–I–B–

'Sinibaldo!'

'I see I have underestimated you.'

The quiet voice from the doorway startled both Falconer and his friend. Neither had heard anyone approaching, and whoever it was had mounted the rickety stairs without creaking a timber. Falconer squinted at the shadowy figure standing in the darkening passage and smiled.

'Come in, poor knight.'

As de Beaujeu stepped forward, Bullock gasped and dropped his hand to the rusty sword that always swung at his waist, more as a threat than an actual weapon. He was afraid that now he needed to use it, and it or he would prove inadequate. The Templar was probably more than a match for himself and the feverish Falconer. He began to draw the ancient weapon from its sheath.

Falconer swiftly but gently stayed his hand, clasping his fingers over Bullock's grasp.

'I think the Templar has come to talk, not fight, Peter.'

He motioned for the man to sit opposite them at the table, and noted the natural grace of his movement. This man was indeed a warrior – a secret warrior trained in the ways of the East. Once a Crusader then. When he spoke, his voice also trod carefully, gently but with a backbone of steel.

'I see you already know of my mission.'

He gestured towards the stolen letter lying on the table between them. Bullock had the good grace to look embarrassed.

'It is true. Master of Cooks Sinibaldo was my contact in the Bishop's household. Shame that he was killed before I could speak to him. But at least you cannot accuse me of being his killer.'

Falconer nodded agreement.

'Let me start from the beginning.'

De Beaujeu explained that his order, the Poor Knights of Christ and the Temple of Solomon as Falconer had surmised, had agreed to carry out a favour for 'certain factions' in Rome representing the Orsini family interests. Bishop Otho was a candidate for the Papacy, but supported by the Orsinis' deadly enemies, the Colonna family. And potentially the English King, of course. The Grand Master of the order learned from his spies that Sinibaldo was jealous of his brother's power and influence, a situation that had been made worse by Otho appointing him Master of Cooks. Sinibaldo had felt mortally offended, but had accepted as it left him in a position to work out his revenge.

'Cain and Abel,' muttered Falconer, remembering his conversation with the Bishop, and thinking that Otho should have listened to his advisers after all. De Beaujeu looked curious at the Master's aside, but continued.

'I was sent by the Grand Master to seek to use Sinibaldo to . . . shall we say, discredit the Bishop. His envy would have been a powerful weapon.'

'And would not have dragged the Orsinis or the Templars directly into the matter,' added Falconer. 'What if that had failed? Would you have killed the Bishop yourself?'

De Beaujeu did not reply, but the answer was in his steady gaze.

'Mine, I think?'

The Templar's right hand reached out and drew the deciphered document towards him, folding it closed. Falconer did not intervene.

'And your transcription of the hidden message?'

Falconer's hand dropped like a dead weight on the incriminating text.

'I think I will keep that for a while. For safety.'

Falconer did not make it clear whose safety he was considering, but de Beaujeu knew that while the secret message was held by Falconer, his own hand was stayed. He got up from the bench with the same lithe power that had gained him access to Aristotle's Hall and was gone. A great sigh of relief burst out of Bullock, as though he had been holding his breath throughout the encounter.

The Regent Master picked up the paper with the Grand Master's message on it and flicked it into the fire. After a moment, the embers blackened the surface, obscuring the letters, then the paper flared up in a yellow flame that lit up the astonished face of Peter Bullock.

'Why did you do that? That paper gave us a hold over him.'

'He needs only to think we have it. Besides, a secret is best kept as a secret.'

Falconer slumped back against the table edge. He felt dizzy, but whether from the fever or the sudden dawning of the truth was difficult to tell.

Chapter Thirteen

Ann Segrim could find no comfort in her herb garden. An entire day had passed since she had left the message with Peter Bullock. Surely Master Falconer had returned to his lodgings by now and received it? Or had the ugly man simply forgotten to pass the message on, assuming that the wishes of a mere woman were unimportant, or concerned with some impropriety? She wished she had reason to travel to Oxford again, but even if she had a good excuse she had barely seen Humphrey to request permission. It galled her that she was a prisoner in her own home, her life ruled by the whim of her husband – especially when he was hardly there himself. Recently he seemed to be either holed up with visitors engaged in conspiratorial conversations, or riding off to God knows where. She crossed herself at the blasphemous use of the Lord's name, even in her thoughts. She must be patient – it had always served her before.

The morning was cool but clear, and the dew tumbled off the fat leaves of the comfrey as she brushed past it. Little beads of water sparkled on the skirt of her plain dress, as though seeding it with pearls. She often found solace in the herb garden, alone and free from the oppressive presence of her husband. She tended the plants lovingly, and took a small delight in dirtying her hands. Indoors she felt like a doll. Careless of the damp and clinging earth, she knelt and began to pick some rue.

'I understand the lady of the manor wishes to speak with me. Perhaps as her servant you could take a message.'

Startled by the sudden appearance of a stranger in her private domain, Ann looked up to correct the man's misunderstanding. It was William Falconer with a broad grin on his face. She rose to her feet, uncaring of the earth that clung to her skirt. Continuing the flirtatious deceit, she dropped a crude curtsey and spoke in the broad accent of her kitchen maid.

'Milady is far too busy to see a common traveller unannounced. Tell me what you want her for.'

Falconer could not suppress a laugh, but it soon turned into a fit of coughing that he could not control. Ann saw for the first time that his face was flushed and sweat was dripping from his forehead. Even if he had walked from Oxford, the morning was still cool and unlikely to raise a sweat in a fit man. She knew he must be ill. Dropping her pretence, she motioned him to a bench by the wall and he gratefully flopped down. She sat hesitantly at the other end of the bench, for the moment retaining a decorous distance from him.

The coughing fit stopped and in response to the unspoken question in her eyes, he spoke.

'It's nothing, just a slight chill. I should not go swimming in the dead of night.'

He clearly was not going to explain this cryptic remark further, and Ann suddenly found herself at a loss for words. She felt foolish, and was aware that his piercing blue eyes, hazed with a fever that she could see was more than a chill, bored into her. She dropped her eyes to her lap, where her hands nervously twisted the folds of her robe. He gently reminded her of her wish to speak to him. Peter Bullock had remembered after all to pass on her message.

Falconer had barely slept in the night – coughing fits and his growing perception of the truth about the murders had conspired to keep him awake. He was sure that Ann Segrim must have another truth to add to the increasing pile that would decipher the puzzle as surely as his knowing the Templar's code. Besides, he simply wanted to see her again. He had risen with the dawn and, despite the hotness coursing through his body, had hurried all the way to Botley, circumventing Oseney Abbey as he did so.

There had been signs of activity in the abbey as the monks rose to their religious observances, but Falconer did not want to enter its gates again until he had spoken to Ann Segrim. And she to him.

Brother John Darby had once more excused himself from the boredom of the daily meeting in the chapter house, and was seated at his desk in the lofty Scriptorium. It was a bright, sunny morning and Brother John's mood suited it. The transcriptions for Master Falconer were nearly completed, and the newest recruit to the team of copyists had managed yesterday to copy a page of text without spilling any ink. Also yesterday he had had a long conversation with Abbot Ralph about the recent mysterious absences of Brother Peter Talam. He expressed his concern that the brother should be so long away when his presence was needed to ensure the regular income from rents for the abbey's properties. He regretted telling tales, but felt the Abbot should know that he had been told by another brother that Brother Peter had travelled as far afield as Wallingford. And hadn't there been trouble at the castle there? Then the night before last he had been abroad when all pious folk were in bed. Ralph had been uncertain what to do, but promised that he would look into the matter.

This very morning, with the early sun warming his heart, Brother John had bumped into the cause of his concern in the corridor connecting the chapel with the Abbot's quarters. The man looked careworn and could hardly muster an excuse as Darby collected the precious parchments that had been knocked out of his grasp on to the stone-flagged floor.

'You could at least help me, Brother,' complained Darby.

Dancing anxiously from one sandal-clad foot to the other, Talam scooped up one of the documents and thrust it abruptly at his colleague.

'Forgive me, Brother, but I have an urgent matter at the hospital.'

With that he was gone, leaving Darby wondering what could be so urgent at St John's. Didn't everyone who got taken there die anyway?

Now he had the extra task of swabbing the dirt from the texts that had been catapulted out of his grasp. Sitting on his high stool he began his day by ensuring they were as pristine as before, then set them aside to carry out his main task. As his copyists silently slid into their allotted seats, he began shaping the large letters that would illuminate the next page of his chronicle. Gradually they spelt out the desired text.

'THE SEVENTH SEAL.'

Falconer hurried back from Botley with the information that Ann Segrim had given him almost completing the assemblage of truths on the murders of both Sinibaldo and poor John Gryffin. The unfortunate student, because he had drawn a bow in Oseney Abbey, was an innocent bystander whose death simply served the ends of the real murderer. Falconer was now nearly sure he knew who that was, and why the murder had been committed. It remained only to trap the man somehow into revealing the truth himself. His head was spinning, but he had to speak to Ralph Harbottle at Oseney. What Ann had told him about Brother Peter Talam meant he must see the Abbot. With each step that he took his feet seemed heavier and heavier. He staggered along the narrow lane that led to the abbey, and a great black cloud of jackdaws and crows rose out of the field to his left. Now he could make out the archway of the abbey, but it seemed to be wobbling and about to collapse. The ground appeared to be shifting under his feet, and he could hardly stand. He couldn't believe there was an earthquake taking place. Not now. But suddenly he was pitched forward into a dark and bottomless pit.

The Seventh Seal

When the Lamb broke the seventh seal, upon the earth was thunder and lightning, and a great earthquake . . .

Falconer's head was splitting with pain and a cacophony of brassy sound was echoing through the vault of his skull, bouncing off the chamber. He squeezed his eyes open, only to see the broken clods of earth into which his face was thrust. He realized he was lying face down on damp and friable soil. Hadn't he collapsed in front of Oseney Abbey on dry and stony ground? And what was causing that horrendous sound? He shakily raised his head from the earth, shifting his hands to his ears to shut out the noise. It was so loud, his teeth seemed to rattle in their sockets. The earth trembled and suddenly pebbles beat upon his back and exposed head. He curled himself into a ball, wrapping his arms over his grizzled locks. Squinting between his elbows at the ground in front of him, he realized the pebbles were hailstones, some the size of his fist, that were crashing to earth into pools of red blood, where they hissed and melted away, turning the glutinous blood into pink rivers that ran between his arms.

Puzzled and a little afraid, he dared to raise his gaze even further, and gasped at the sight of seven monstrous forms that towered almost beyond his vision into the clouds above. It was as though they had been inhumanly stretched on a rack, their feet still stuck to the ground and their heads now in the sky – a sky that roiled with colours and cloud shapes, sometimes resembling fire-breathing dragons, sometimes gentle flocks of sheep. One of the towering forms, white and rippling, like a column supporting the heavens themselves, raised a gilded trumpet to its lips. Again the piercing blast split through Falconer's brain, and for a moment it seemed as though he was curled up inside his own skull peering out of the sightless sockets. The ever-changing hues of the sky were darkened by a massive shape that whistled and roared as it approached. A fiery mountain ripped from its earthly chains descended on him erupting gouts of molten rock. In a few moments it obscured the whole sky, and he screamed as the edifice of his skull was shattered by the unimaginable weight of earth pressing on it from above.

There was nothing to hear but the echo of the last blast on the heavenly trumpet dinning in his ears. His eyes blinked open as he felt the soothing to-and-fro motion of a boat beneath his feet. He gasped as he realized he was not dead after all. But he could not understand how he came to be aboard ship. It must be ten years since he was last on a boat, travelling back through the Mediterranean from Cyprus – unless the last ten years had been some strange dream, and had not really occurred at all. He urgently needed to make sense of what had happened to him. If it was all a dream, the final act had been terrifying. He sat up in the bunk in which he had been lying and called out. No one answered. Instead there came a thundering sound, and the boards of the boat beneath his feet began to shudder and vibrate. It was as though some underwater monster was bearing down upon the boat, intent on swallowing it up. He staggered out on to the deck to witness a great white column burst from the sea amidst a fountain of spray. Around its base the water boiled and seethed, and great waves were thrown back from it. Falconer grasped the side of the boat as the mighty torrent struck, tossing the tiny vessel high into the air and dropping it with spine-jolting suddenness back into the fretful sea.

The column formed into another angel, for that was what those monster shapes surely were, and a living trumpet sprouted from its lips blaring out its apocalyptic message. Suddenly, Falconer was aware of other vessels in the sea around him, some already shattered by the pounding waves. Sailors clung to spars and broken timbers, bobbing like discarded rubbish on the surface of the choppy sea. A cacophony of screams ripped at the tatters of his rain, and the blinding light of a shooting star flew across the firmament straight towards the unfortunate seafarers. Its passage over his head was accompanied by a thunderous roar that seemed to split the sky, and it splashed down into the sea amidst a plume of steam. As the boiling waters settled, the sea around where the star had sunk was stained an evil and slimy green. The miasma spread across the surface of the sea in a shimmering slick, and the men who had been pitched from their boats were sucked into it and swallowed without trace, their screams cut off as they disappeared below its turbid surface.

The flimsy boat that was all that stood between Falconer and certain death in the poisoned sea began to rock violently in the choppy waves. Each surge threatened to toss him over the side. Then he heard the sound of shingle under the keel of his little craft, and almost fell over the side of the boat in his haste to regain firm ground. His feet hit pebbles and he stumbled badly, rolling on his back and cracking his head. He let the rounded stones press into his hips and the back of his skull, unmindful of the pain, glad only to be alive. He kept his eyes tight shut as he heard the fourth trumpet sound, opening them when he felt a frightening coldness rolling over his feet and legs. He looked down into nothingness.

In panic he looked up at the sky, momentarily imagining he could see a face that somehow resembled the craggy features of Peter Bullock. He thought wryly that if God had a human face, there was every reason that it should be Peter Bullock's. But then part of the face became obscured, and he couldn't discern it at all. Part of the sky – sun, moon and stars in the one firmament – was black. No, not black, it simply wasn't there. Almost against his will, his eyes were drawn down to his legs, which now felt icy cold. They had disappeared too. He could not find the words to describe what he saw. Over his lower limbs lay a darkness that seemed to swallow the light, and it crept ever higher up his legs as he lay there watching the horror. Realizing the danger, he squealed in terror and dragged himself away from the encroaching dark. With relief he saw that his legs and feet were still there, though they felt numb and cold.

Awkwardly he staggered to his feet, and stumbled over the shifting surface of the shingle. He moved inland to get away from the shipwrecked mariners and enveloping darkness. He crested the shingle dunes and gazed over barren desert dotted with grey boulders. Before his unbelieving eyes, a massive crack opened up, zigzagging across the parched and brittle earth, and sulphurous fumes assailed his nostrils. Coughing and choking, Falconer dropped to his knees, holding on to the shifting earth beneath his feet as it ground and shattered. Every moment was a struggle for survival, and every moment brought a new horror. He heard a buzzing noise like the sound of a huge swarm of bees. As he raised his eyes to the heavens, the rasping grew in intensity, setting his teeth on edge, and he grimaced with pain. Out of the cavernous wound in the desert's surface rose a myriad tiny winged shapes. In their buzzing they spoke the name of their master – Abbadon the Destroyer. They rose and rose like smoke from a fiery furnace, eventually blotting out most of the mottled sky with their presence. Falconer was trapped between the encroaching nothingness and a plague of locusts.

Looking around him he realized that the rounded shapes he had thought were boulders were in fact people burrowing in terror into the unrelenting soil. They wailed in fear as, like Falconer, they cast their gaze up to the living clouds of insects now descending on them. In an instant Falconer and the other wretches were smothered in the creatures. He frantically began to brush them from his arms and head. It was then he knew they were no ordinary locusts. On top of each chitinous green body was a tiny human head with long flowing locks. As the creatures grinned at his pain and fear, between their lips he could see jagged, pointed teeth running with blood. He felt sharp, painful pricks all over his body and, picking one of the locusts from his arm, he could see it was armed with a scorpion's tail that plunged time and time again into his frail flesh. He redoubled his furious efforts to sweep the horrific creatures from his body and stamp on them. He could hear the crunching as they died but as soon as he had brushed one arm free and begun on the other, even more locusts replaced those he had crushed. He was drowning in insects as surely as those seafarers had in water. The exquisite pain of thousands of tiny stings was too much to bear, and he blacked out.

When he came to, he appeared to be lying on a soft bed looking up into a cavernous room. His eyes still swam, and vague shapes hovered over him, dissolving and reforming like scudding clouds. The face of a mighty angel, its features distorted but discernibly those of Ann Segrim, descended from the heavens and spoke in a tongue he could not understand. The words echoed around his skull like distant thunder. He strove to rise but his limbs were dead, refusing to obey him. He could see a scroll in the hands of the mighty angel, who bestrode his bed with feet of fire. Further away a voice from the heavens told him what to do. It said:

'Take the scroll in the angel's hand, and eat it. Take and eat it. Although it will taste honeyed in your mouth, it will feel bitter in your stomach.'

Weakly, Falconer allowed the scroll to be placed in his mouth. At first it tasted sweet, but as it slid down to his stomach he felt a sour taste overwhelming the first sensation. He fell back and slept.

In his dreams he saw a hugely pregnant woman, robed in sparkling colours that resembled the sun and stars. She floated in the sky as though she weighed nothing, yet her stomach was distended with the child she screamed to deliver. Into the edge of Falconer's vision swam another portent. It was a great red dragon with seven heads on long thin necks that weaved in and out of each other. Each head was topped with horns that threatened to pierce the distended flesh of the gravid woman. Each beastly head drooled and slavered in anticipation of the birth, for the dragon clearly aimed to devour the new-born. But at the moment of the birth the hand of God scooped up the mewling child, still covered in its mother's fluids, and set it at his right hand. The several heads of the dragon roared in anguish at their lost prey, one chewing at the neck of its neighbour. Foul gobbets of blood and flesh flew across the sky, spattering on to Falconer's face. He recoiled in horror, and woke up.

He was kneeling in a crowd of worshippers before a stone altar. Around him everyone was chanting in low tones that he could not understand. The mood was sombre, and he raised his eyes to the priest who stood before the altar with his back to the congregation. The priest seemed to loom large over the kneeling worshippers and was raising a chalice over his head. Falconer felt a sense of foreboding, and could not tear his gaze from the priest as he turned towards the crowd. The man's head was riven with a jagged, suppurating wound, as though it had been cleaved by a massive axe. And what a face it was beneath the wound. There was nothing human about it at all – it was the face of the Beast. Falconer felt his arms being bound to his side as the fiendish congregation pressed around him, their hot, foetid breath on his neck and cheeks. The Beast advanced on him holding out a cat-like paw instead of a hand. A viciously sharp claw flicked out as Falconer's head was pulled back, exposing his pulsing neck. As he felt the prick of the claw upon his flesh, he heard the sound of heavenly voices in prayer, and his eyes flicked open.

At first he thought he was dead and in the presence of God. For the face that hovered over him resembled that of Peter Bullock, and he remembered his earlier encounter with God, bearing the constable's face. Then he saw the face split with a worldly grin, and realized he was back in the land of the living. Nervously he cast about the room in which he lay, half-expecting it to dissolve into another nightmare. But it remained stubbornly solid, and the voice of Peter Bullock was reassuringly normal.

'I see you are with us once again.'

Chapter Fourteen

'The Austins found you at the doors of their abbey. You were raving and feverish. They said you had the ague and were as likely to die as recover. That's why they brought you here.'

Bullock sat beside the low truckle bed on which lay a weakened and exhausted Falconer. They were in one of the cubicles in St John's Hospital outside East Gate. The plain wooden screening around the bed finished just above head height, and beyond it Falconer could make out one of the arched trusses that supported the lofty ceiling. The upper reaches of the hall were lost in darkness, and the walls of the cubicle pressed in on Falconer like the sides of a coffin. There was a smell of vomit and stale sweat that he felt sure was not all his own. As if in confirmation, a low-pitched groaning came from the cubicle to his left.

Bullock saw the direction of Falconer's gaze.

'The half-dead disease,' he murmured. Falconer shook his head sadly, knowing of the evil, slippery humour that rendered one side of the body powerless and turned the face into a distorted mask. It came mostly to those of fuller years – fifty or more – but sometimes attacked younger men. Not many recovered from it, and those who did were often useless creatures shuffling through their miserable life. Though he had only just awoken, he decided he would be glad to be out of this depressing place.

He tried to sit up but fell back exhausted. Bullock urged him to rest as he had been at death's door only a few hours before. It was now night, and Falconer had been in the grip of the ague for almost two days. Bullock explained that he had been at Falconer's bedside most of that time – and when he wasn't, Ann Segrim had played the role of an angel of mercy. Recalling some of the horror of his nightmares, Falconer knew that she had indeed been an angel in his fevered brain. He thought he might reserve for another time the revelation of his vision of Peter Bullock as the face of God.

'Two days!'

Falconer was suddenly aware of what Bullock had just said. The accursed fever had wasted too much time, just when he was anxious to put his deductive work to the ultimate test. He needed to take action now. But he was so feeble that lifting his head was like hefting a ponderous rock at arm's length, and brought him out in a sweat. He would need Bullock's help. And that of a few others too.

'You said that Mistress Segrim was here?'

'Yes, she wanted to talk to you the day you disappeared, remember?'

'And I went to see her.'

'Well, she was in town for the market yesterday and went to Aristotle's to seek you out again. Young Hugh Pett told her you were ill, and where you were.'

Bullock's face split in a salacious grin.

'You clearly exercise a powerful influence over the lady. She was most concerned at your state. Even helped to wipe your fevered brow, and encouraged you to take some of the medicine the apothecary prepared.'

Falconer half-recalled the scroll that God in his dream had encouraged him to eat, and the bitter aftertaste rose in his gorge again. The memory was sweetened by the thought that Mistress Ann had been seeking him. After their talk in the herb garden, there could be no more urgent information for her to impart. She must have been seeking him out for his own sake. His fevered mind rapidly constructed an imagined courtship – the knowledge that she was married, and to Humphrey Segrim, was but a minor complication. But first he must solve the mystery of the murders.

How could he bring matters to a head, when he was so enfeebled and not able even to rise from his sickbed?

Falconer realized Bullock was still speaking.

'I'm sorry, my friend, what did you say?'

'That she has left her servant to wait on your recovery, so that she might be informed as soon as possible that you were out of danger. Or that you were dead,' he added cheerily.

The first light of a new dawn filtered through the blood-red glass in the high arched window of the main hall of the hospital. Its rays crept across the dark stained-wood panels of Falconer's cubicle like blood dribbling from an ethereal creature, the vital fluids of some ghostly being that might have escaped from Falconer's apocalyptic nightmare. A quiet smile crossed his strained and pale features.

'You said that I have been in a stupor for two days. What does that make today?'

Bullock had to ponder on that question. To him the days ran one into the next. As a child he had worked as a farm labourer and the hours of the day were regulated by the rising and setting of the sun, the year by the seasons of growth and harvesting. Even as a soldier, his time had been ordered by the seasons, for no one wanted to fight through rain and mud. Now in this crowded city of souls who earned their living by exercising only their minds, natural cycles were unimportant. Masters and students lived a life divorced from the real world he had known, following an artifice of time that split days into hours. Terce, sext and nones were for quibbling monks and masters. But each day he grew more like them and away from his past. He shrugged and calculated in his head.

'The last day of the month of March.'

'Good, I am not too late, then.'

'For what?'

Falconer ignored his question and, clasping his hands together behind his head, leaned back in triumph on the sweat-soaked mattress.

'You must go to Aristotle's Hall. In the chest in my room you will find a bundle of papers. Bring me the top one. No, bring me them all, then I can be sure I have the one I want.'

Bullock rose to go, his limbs cracking from having sat so long. But Falconer, staring into space, continued to give his instructions.

'After that you must ask old Richard de Sotell something.'

Bullock was puzzled. 'The Friar-Senior of the Dominicans?'

'The same. He must arrange for our good ranting Friar Fordam to come to my bedside. And it must be before terce tomorrow – the time is vital. Then send Mistress Ann's servant to me. I want him to take a message of more than my good health to her.'

Humphrey Segrim rose late that morning feeling particularly cheerful. He felt sure that his little game with Master Falconer had proved effective. It had been a risk, because he had not told his co-conspirators, who he felt sure would not have agreed to his actions. In their high circles, someone in Falconer's position was like a horse-fly causing their mount to rear and plunge. The simple, effective solution was to swat it mightily out of existence. When Chancellor-to-be de Cantilupe had failed them, their limited patience with the subtle approach had run out. They were all for killing the Regent Master, with his bothersome buzzing around the flanks of their plotting. And Segrim knew whose task it would have been to arrange the killing – if not to carry it out personally. That was fine for those nobles, who travelled around the country following the royal progress of their monarch and living off the fat of other people's land. He had to live in the vicinity of Oxford, and the death of a Regent Master, even one so vexatious as William Falconer, would stir up endless trouble.

No, he was glad he had put Falconer off the scent in such a spectacular way. After all, who could question the word of the King of England? He yawned and, idly scratching his chest through the heavy cloth of his nightgown, crossed to the window that overlooked the courtyard of his manor house. The sun was well up, and he was pleased to see his servants scurrying around the yard ensuring everything was arranged for the comfortable progress of their master through the day. He spotted his wife's personal manservant, Sekston, hurrying up the track from the direction of Oxford. He wondered where the man had been so early, and recalled he had not seen him around the previous day when Ann had returned from the Oxford market. She had seemed agitated over something, and had closed her door on him. Not wishing to destroy his good mood, he had turned to the company of a fine wine from Poitou rather than a sour wife.

Now Sekston was crossing the courtyard towards the front door, and Segrim pressed his face against the diamond shapes of the window glass to see who he was going to speak to. He could just make out the top of his wife's head as she took a few paces down the front steps. Sekston spoke earnestly, then turned away to carry on with his normal tasks. If Segrim had been able to see more than the top of his wife's head, he would have seen the look of relief and joy on her face caused by the news from St John's Hospital.

He was once again confronted by the pregnant woman. She swam before his eyes, alluring in all her gravid beauty. The scent of her glowing body assailed his nostrils and he felt a stirring in his loins. As she turned her head towards him, he realized it was Ann Segrim. Damp strands of hair stuck to her brow, and her face was flushed. She was holding his hand firmly in hers, and squeezing it each time a spasm wracked her stomach. Suddenly the smile of joy fell from her features, as she looked over his shoulder. He felt the fiery breath on his neck, and knew without looking that the evil dragon was behind him – a demon with Humphrey Segrim's face. He felt the icy claw of the monster resting on his bare arm.

Waking with a start, he saw the incongruously cheery face of John Darby hovering over him. Falconer cast an anxious glance around the cubicle, fearful that the solid wood of the panelling would dissolve into another nightmare. Darby's face bore a look of puzzlement and anxiety mixed.

'I was told you were recovered, but you still seem far from well. Perhaps I should go.'

Falconer grasped the dry, cold hand that still lay across his arm, glad it was fleshy and not made of scales and claws.

'No, stay. It was just a bad dream.'

He drew himself up out of the clammy coverings and leaned against the wooden wall. From the angle of the light cast through the window, he deduced that he had slept well into the afternoon.

'What brings you here?'

'Concern for a friend, of course. But I do have something to show you that might improve your spirits.'

He dug his hands into a large leather satchel at his feet and drew out a heavy tome. The cords binding it were neatly executed, and the leather casing was fresh and shiny. The pleasant smell of it aroused the curiosity of the Regent Master. Darby turned it reverently in his hands so that the front cover faced Falconer. He smiled and took it from the monk.

'Open it.'

Falconer did so in anticipation, and the pages crackled with newness. He read the opening sheaf with its lovingly hand-inscribed, illuminated letters.

'*De Partibus Animalium*. It's my text of Aristotle, but I did not ask for it to be bound.'

'A gift from me. You will find the main text is executed legibly, if a little plainly. Brother Adam is skilful but not an artist. I thought to improve it myself with an opening page. And then it demanded to be bound.'

Darby had obviously intended to please Falconer with his embellishments. The Regent Master did not have the heart to explain that the accuracy of the text was all he desired, and thanked him for his efforts.

'I will cherish it as the outward sign of a good friendship.'

The rosy-cheeked monk added a blush to his already rubicund features, and bent down to remove the original of the copied text from his satchel. Unlike its copy, this book was worn and old, the cover cracked from excessive use. He passed it over to Falconer, and out of curiosity asked where the text came from that Falconer so prized.

'The rabbi Jehozadok. It is a text taken directly from the Greek, without it filtering through half a dozen other languages. Have you read it? There's a fascinating section on how sharks roll over on their backs to eat. The shark is a fish, you know . . .'

Falconer hesitated when he saw the frown on the monk's face. His own enthusiasm for Aristotle and scientific study of the world often made him forget that others deemed such observation an affront to God. Perhaps Brother John felt so, or perhaps he disapproved of Falconer's friendship with a Jew. He hoped it was not the latter. The awkward silence was broken by another voice.

'You are tiring Master Falconer. I suggest you leave now.'

The doorway of the little cubicle was filled with the tall figure of another monk. Brother Peter Talam's stern rebuke caused Darby to throw an amused look heavenwards. He picked up his satchel from the floor and silently bowed out of the room, casting a conspiratorial wink at Falconer over Talam's shoulder as he left. Brother Peter waited patiently for Darby to leave before he spoke.

'You are still far from well, so I have brought you a remedy. I prepared it myself.'

From the voluminous sleeve of his habit he produced a small, stoppered flask and bent over the prostrate Falconer. The bright and staring look in his eyes filled William with unease. The monk uncorked the flask and held it out imperiously.

'You must drink it now.'

Falconer took the flask hesitantly and sniffed the brew. It smelled foul, as though some small creature had crawled into the flask to die – a long time ago. He recoiled, but the firm hands of Talam clasped his and pressed the flask up to his lips. The monk nodded in encouragement, as Falconer's mind raced to find a way to avoid drinking the potion. He was too weak to fight off the monk on his own. He could think of no excuse, and the cold rim of the flask was at his mouth. Visions of the Last Judgement flashed through his mind, and he gagged at the merest taste of the brew as it touched his tongue. The monk's grip relaxed for a moment and Falconer coughed chestily.

'That smells awful. No wonder it is making you cough.'

The constable's voice cut through the tension in the room, and Falconer offered up a silent prayer at the return of Peter Bullock. He carefully pushed the flask and its contents away from his lips.

'I must ask you to leave us alone, Brother Talam. I have a confidential matter to discuss with the constable.'

The tall monk straightened up, towering over the prostrate Falconer. There was a thunderous look in his eyes as he stared at the Regent Master, and he carefully pressed the cap into the neck of the flask.

'I will return later, then.'

Pushing angrily past Bullock, he stormed out of the little cubicle. Both men could hear his sandalled feet slapping on the stone floor of the hospital as he retreated. Falconer glanced up at the questioning look on the face of his old comrade.

'I will explain it all later. Now give me the papers.'

Bullock offered the battered bundle of documents he had removed from the chest in Falconer's room at Aristotle's Hall. To him they were an unimpressive pile of tattered pages, even though he was normally in awe of any learned texts. Reading was not his strong point, and any words that were inscribed on paper must be powerful. But some of this writing was on tiny scraps with every inch of the surface covered in lines and spirals of words. Perhaps their power lay in the symbols they formed, and the hidden meanings they foretold. Certainly Falconer was handling them reverently as if they were some necromancer's lodestone.

Bullock sat on the side of the bed as Falconer shuffled through the papers and drew from the cord binding them one which he held closely to his eyes. He read it carefully, turning it towards the light that now edged higher and higher up the panelled wall as the day drew on. If he had remembered the text correctly, he had precious little time left. Then he saw it and mumbled excitedly to himself, tracing his finger along the sentence written by Roger Bacon in some Franciscan prison of a cell far away in France.

'*Eclipsis solis – Kal. Aprilis in fine quarti mensis Arabum feria vi. hora diei iii.*'

Bullock interrupted his evident pleasure.

'I spoke to de Sotell and he said he would send the friar to you tomorrow morning early. Couldn't see why you would want to set eyes on him again, mind you. And neither do I.'

Falconer smiled mysteriously.

'You will find out. You see, I am convinced I know who killed Sinibaldo, and John Gryffin. I just need Humphrey Segrim to confirm it for me.'

'Segrim knows?'

'Yes. It was his plotting that resulted in their deaths.'

'But I thought you said the other day that you had been convinced Segrim was not involved.'

Falconer sat up and clutched at his friend's sleeve.

'Yes, but that was when I thought the aim was to kill Bishop Otho. When I thought, foolishly, that Sinibaldo's death had been a tragic accident. And Segrim had no reason to kill the Bishop – the very opposite in fact. But the death wasn't an accident. Sinibaldo was the intended victim all along.'

Falconer's eyes sparkled at this revelation, but Bullock was now completely lost.

'How do you work that out?'

'From what our friendly Templar and his message told. And a few other clues I observed for myself.'

The constable was about to ask Falconer to explain what

clues, but the Regent Master pressed on oblivious of Bullock's confusion.

'Until then I had been blind, or at least looking at the facts as if in some fine lady's pretty mirror. They were there all right, in front of my eyes, but they were all back to front. Left was right, and right was left. All I had to do was turn round . . .'

Holding his arm in a vice-like grip, Falconer spun the unsuspecting constable completely round so that he faced out of the cubicle.

'And there behind me was reality, not the mirror's reflection.'

Both men continued to talk in conspiratorial tones as Falconer laid his plans for the next morning. Neither heard the soft stirring of a sandalled foot, as a monkish figure slunk away from the other side of the thin panelling and disappeared into the gathering gloom of the evening.

Chapter Fifteen

With dawn barely broken, all was bedlam in the courtyard of Botley Manor. Several servants ran hither and thither, hastily preparing the best horse in the stables for their master. Hardly had the groom led the skittish horse out, when Humphrey Segrim ran down the steps from the main hall and mounted in a panic. A conversation with his wife the previous evening had shattered his complacency, and now he did not know what to do for the best. He lashed out with his boot at the groom who held his bucking horse, and the man let go of the reins in terror. Segrim yanked hard on the freed reins and spurred the mount towards Oseney Abbey, the words of his wife ringing in his head.

Humphrey had barely completed his meal yesterday, revelling in the taste of the boiled venison well seasoned with sage, pepper, cloves and mace, when she had spoiled it all. He was taking a deep draught of Rhenish wine, when she announced she had news of Master Falconer in Oxford.

'He has been very ill with an ague, but is now recovering.'

'Pity,' mumbled Segrim into the depths of his pewter goblet. Ann gave him a hard look, so he responded more generously.

'I am glad to hear it. But why should this little clerk's health be of concern to me?'

'He is no mere clerk, but a very clever man. It is said he knows who killed Bishop Otho's brother. That it is someone of considerable power. Someone who may even be linked with the King.'

Segrim paled and the luscious Rhenish turned to ashes in his throat. He sought to correct the prattlings of his wife.

'No, no. You must have misheard the tale. The King could not be involved. It was some scurvy clerk, who hanged himself in prison at Wallingford Castle.'

Ann lowered her eyes, as if dutifully reluctant to contradict her husband. But contradict him she did.

'Apparently the clerk, God rest him, was also the victim of the same murderer. I heard it from my servant, Sekston, who has it from the constable no less. Master Falconer plans to reveal all to the proper authorities at terce tomorrow.'

She paused and stared with large, artless eyes at her husband.

'I wonder who the someone in high authority can be?'

Humphrey slumped back in his chair, the half-digested meat sitting in his stomach like a stone.

Nor had he felt any better this morning, after a night spent tossing and turning over the best way to deal with Falconer. He had even been unaware of his wife at her bedroom window as he berated the groom for his clumsy preparation of his horse. There was a smile of satisfaction on her face. As he raced through the chilly dawn, he thought perhaps murder was the only avenue open to him now. God, how one killing piled on another when a thread of conspiracy was being woven. At least he did not have to sully his own hands. He turned his lathered horse into the courtyard of Oseney Abbey just as the bells rang for prime.

William Falconer was getting nervous. Everything that he planned depended on accurate timing. Segrim and his accomplice must be enticed to St John's before terce for his plan to work, for nothing could delay the inevitable movement of the spheres on which he was relying. He hoped that Ann Segrim had spun a sufficiently attractive tale to ensure her husband's arrival. Whether the other one would come depended on Segrim's own persuasion. And his conviction that Falconer already knew everything. As the time approached, Falconer became more and more uncertain that he did.

The first rays of the sun were probing weakly through the window and tracking slowly down the darkly panelled wall of the cubicle where Falconer still lay. Anxious for everything to work, he stretched across to the thin wall dividing him from the next cubicle where the unfortunate with the half-dead disease had lain. It had been late in the night that his luck had improved, and he had expired. Better to rest in God than halfway between heaven and earth. Two novices had quietly removed his mortal remains for Christian burial, while the rest of the hospital slept. The cubicle was now occupied by two very live human beings. Falconer rapped on the wall and the muffled voice of Peter Bullock responded, confirming his presence. The other voice was more reluctant to respond but, after some urging from the constable, it rang out loud and clear.

Falconer was as satisfied as he could be, though the passage of time marked by the progress of the shaft of light down the panelling gave him cause for concern. Would Segrim and his accomplice be here soon enough? The sad chorus of quiet moans and coughs from the other inhabitants of the hospital punctuated the air, depressing Falconer's usual optimism even more. Could he detect a change in the quality of the light already? If they did not come soon his plan would not work. As if in reassurance, the beam of light brightened as a cloud cleared the sun. But still it crept inexorably down the wall to the point of no return. Falconer lay back on his pillow and sighed.

'You do not look well, Master Falconer.'

The voice roused him from his doze. How long had he slept? A few moments, or too long? He looked at the mote of light – it was still high on the wall, so all was well. Humphrey Segrim's portly figure filled the archway of the cubicle, his arm holding the heavy curtain to one side. Falconer sighed a sort of agreement with his observation, and raised his hand weakly as if to beckon the man in. Was he on his own after all? Falconer thought he saw a drably clad figure behind him, but the curtain dropped across the arch and cut off his view. He would have to proceed with just Segrim, then – and hope the other was present.

The man took the few steps forward that brought him to Falconer's bedside and lowered his bulk on the edge of the truckle bed. It creaked under the weight and Segrim half-rose in alarm. Falconer took his arm in reassurance and drew Segrim towards him.

'Please, you will have to come close, my hearing is not good.'

His voice seemed feeble to Segrim, and he wondered if he needed to make an end of the man or if Nature would carry out the deed soon anyway. Come what may, it was good that Falconer was in such a state. For even if Nature had to be assisted, no one would question his demise. But whatever happened, his death should come soon. If Ann was to be believed, Falconer intended to tell what he knew this very morning. Segrim wished only to satisfy his curiosity about how much Falconer knew, and how he came to know it. Then he would arrange to stifle the knowledge for ever. He was also anxious to know why the secret 'audience' with the King had not put him off the track. It had seemed to do so at the time.

Falconer appeared to be reading his mind, and spoke in a low, hoarse tone.

'You must repent of what you did, before it is too late.'

Segrim looked anxiously into the sick man's piercing blue eyes. They appeared full of warning and their own terror.

'What do you mean? Too late?'

Falconer clutched his arm in a grip of iron, far too strong for the grip of a sick man. Something awful seemed to be driving him.

'Before the Final Judgement.'

The words Falconer spoke hung in the air between the two men. Suddenly Segrim was aware of a terrifying voice echoing in the rafters above his head. It spoke of the breaking of the Seven Seals of the Book of Judgement. Disaster piled on disaster as the terrible voice predicted the end of the world.

'At the breaking of the seventh seal, seven angels prepared to blow seven trumpets calling horrors unimaginable down on the earth. At the first trump hail and fire mingled with red blood scythed down on the earth and a third of all growing things were burned. At the second trump a burning mountain plunged into the sea and a third of the waters turned to blood, killing a third of all creatures living in it. The third angel blew and a great star named Wormwood fell from the sky, poisoning the rivers and streams.'

There was a pause, and even Falconer, who knew what was about to happen, felt a shiver of fear course up his spine. Segrim was transfixed. The disembodied voice continued.

'When the fourth angel blew his trumpet, a third part of the sky was struck. A third part of the moon and the stars, and the sun. So the sky went dark, and the light of the sun failed.'

Segrim read the look in Falconer's eyes and followed his gaze up to the light falling through the high arch of the window above them. To Segrim's dismay the light seemed to be failing, and he jerked up from the bed to see the orb of the sun filtered through the red-stained glass. There was a great bite out of one side, as though something was consuming it. He wanted to cry in horror, but a strangled whimper was all he could force out of his throat. The maniacal voice of warning continued inexorably.

'Woe, woe, woe to the dwellers on the earth . . .'

Ignoring the litany, Falconer dragged Segrim back down until their faces were inches apart.

'Confess now before it is too late. You killed Sinibaldo, didn't you? And John Gryffin.'

Segrim wailed and sought to free himself from this demon that confronted him. But Falconer's grip was too firm. He could not escape the piercing gaze which was but a reflection of the scrutiny he would face at the end of the world. He could dissimulate no more, and the truth forced itself out of his constricted throat.

'No, no. Please, it was not I who killed them. Yes, I arranged their deaths, may God forgive me. But I did not actually kill them.'

'Then, who did?'

Segrim cast a nervous glance back at the curtain of the cubicle. He hesitated, but still the disembodied voice predicting the end assailed his ears.

'The falling star opened up the abyss, and from it a plume of smoke, like that from a fiery furnace, filled the sky obscuring the sun.'

Segrim's gaze switched to the window where the sun was indeed half-obscured, as though by a thick pall of smoke. Falconer pulled the jowly face down close to his own. The man was quivering in terror, his eyes rolling in his head as he weighed God's retribution against a human one. Falconer spat the question at him.

'Who killed them?'

In the gloom of the cubicle, robbed of the sun's natural rays by the solar eclipse predicted accurately by Roger Bacon several years earlier, Falconer sensed another presence. A hooded figure resembling Death hovered at Segrim's shoulder, and cast something over his head. Suddenly Segrim's bulk bore down on him, pinning him to the bed. The man's eyes bulged as though they would start out of his head. His voice was reduced to a throaty gargle and his mouth dropped open, dribbling saliva over Falconer. His fat fingers clutched at his throat, trying to release what seemed to be a string of beads embedded in the fleshy folds of his neck.

In his weakened state Falconer could not thrust aside Segrim's squirming body. Whoever was strangling him was bearing his own weight down on Segrim's back, pinning Falconer beneath them both. His arms became entangled in the ruck of bedcovers, and he stared helplessly at the bloated face of the dying man pushed obscenely down against his own. He watched as the spark of Segrim's life began to fade in his eyes, only then coming to his senses enough to cry out a warning to Peter Bullock in the next cubicle, his voice no more than a feeble squeak.

With a roar, Bullock pushed Friar Fordam to one side, cutting off his apocalyptic monologue, and lurched through the archway of the cubicle they occupied next to Falconer's. He emerged just as a hooded figure departed from where Falconer lay. Fearing the worst for his friend, he hesitated about whether he should attend to his needs or stop the fugitive. In that moment, the man charged into him and, knocking Bullock off balance, fled past and out into the penumbral gloom.

Bullock picked himself up and anxiously lifted the curtain of Falconer's cubicle. For a moment he thought he was too late, for the large frame of a man lay face down across the bed. Then he realized the body was garbed in the sort of rich clothes that Falconer never wore – and he heard the Regent Master's curse.

'Get him off me.'

Bullock lifted the dead weight of Humphrey Segrim off his friend, who sucked some air into his lungs. Falconer swung his legs off the bed and stood up, still appalled at his own incapacity. The room swam and he clutched at the wall for support. Then he saw the grotesque doll-like figure clutched in Bullock's hefty arms.

'Lay him down on the bed.'

Bullock, still clutching the inert form, thought his friend mad. And who wouldn't be, who had lived through the last few moments? It was all insane – from the ravings of the Dominican to the disappearance of the sun. Falconer grasped him by the shoulder.

'He may still live.'

Shaking his head Bullock rolled Segrim's body on to the truckle bed that had been Falconer's refuge for three days, and stood back as his friend approached the corpse. He looked on in alarm as Falconer bunched his fists together above his head and brought them down with unmerciful force on Segrim's chest.

'If he wasn't dead before, that will ensure he is now.'

Falconer merely grunted, and repeated his assault on the dead man. At this attack, there was a sharp intake of breath from the apparent corpse. For Bullock it was another miracle in a day of miracles. Like Lazarus, Segrim began to breathe again though his chest rose fitfully and feebly. Falconer eased the man's head back and drew something from the folds of his beefy neck. He held it up for Bullock to see, who identified it immediately.

'It's a rosary.'

'Yes, and the very instrument that killed John Gryffin.'

He rolled the individual beads through his fingers.

'Remember those circular bruises around his neck?'

'And I let him go,' cursed Bullock, smashing one meaty fist into the other palm.

'Oh, don't worry. I know who it was.'

The constable knew it would be too easy for Falconer merely to give him a name. The man was infuriating.

'And I think I know where he'll be.'

He looked up thoughtfully to the spill of light through the glazed window, as the sun returned to its normal state.

The monks in Oseney Abbey were still perturbed by the eclipse of the sun. Ralph Harbottle had chivvied the older brothers of the order back to their everyday tasks. But some of the younger ones still exchanged excited opinions in hushed tones as their errands caused their paths to cross. Therefore the arrival of a gaunt and tired Regent Master was little noticed. William Falconer had walked the length of a busy Oxford, and left through the postern gate he had taken on the fateful day of the master cook's murder. A journey on foot that was nothing to him a few days ago now taxed his weakened limbs to the limit. He had insisted that Peter Bullock stay behind, that he could tackle this last step in his investigation by himself. But now he wondered whether he was being foolish. In this state he could not defend himself if his adversary became violent. But shrugging aside his doubts, he pushed himself away from the smooth yellow stone of the archway where he leaned and crossed the courtyard. He knew where the monk would be. Did he not visit his lair every time he came to pay his rent?

'The year 1261. The quarrel continues between King Henry and the barons because he refuses to observe the Provisions of Oxford. On Ash Wednesday terrible lightning and thunder was heard at Westminster. Pope Alexander IV died on 20 March. A dispute broke out at Oseney between the Papal Legate and some students. The Legate's brother has been killed and the students imprisoned at Wallingford. One of the incarcerated hanged himself, and accepted the guilt for Sinibaldo's death. Sanchia, Queen of Germany has died. There was an eclipse of the sun on Friday, 1st April at the end of the fourth month of the Hegira, at the third hour of the day.'

When the doors of the Scriptorium crashed open, revealing a tired but determined Regent Master of the University, Brother John Darby raised his eyes from the elaborately illuminated page of the abbey chronicle. Completing it today was a source of satisfaction to him. Now it mattered not that his pursuer was standing before him. He had not been at all surprised to see him there – the man was so stubborn and persistent that a close encounter with death would not deter him. A soft smile played over his lips. Falconer had survived his own death, only to come face to face with someone else's. He would have liked to stare into the eyes of Segrim himself when he despatched him. But the opportunity offered him at St John's Hospital had been too tempting. Besides, he had no feelings for Humphrey Segrim – the man had been foolish and vain, and deserved to die.

The monk slowly closed the book in front of him and stepped down from his dais. He walked the length of the Scriptorium between the desks of the other scribes. Every one had been trained painstakingly by him, and he was proud of their work. His work and God's work. The tall and weakened figure of the Regent Master awaited him in the doorway. He could detect a stirring of curiosity in the others in the room. They knew something unusual was afoot, but their discipline, instilled by him, kept their heads lowered over the texts they copied. As he reached the doorway, Falconer stepped back and he walked through, gently closing the two halves of the oaken door on his domain. Behind it he could hear a rising tide of whispers.

Brother John leaned back against the heavy doors and sighed.

'How did you know it was me?'

Falconer smiled, his pallid face lighting up with pleasure.

'I didn't until the very last. Or at least I couldn't be sure. Segrim has not the force of will to commit cold-blooded murder, and anyway he was in the presence of the Bishop when Sinibaldo was killed. I checked that with the Bishop himself. The two servants who were in the kitchen at his death were not capable of such a deed. That left me with a puzzle, until I realized who I was forgetting. The very persons you never take note of in a monastery.'

'The monks.'

'Exactly. You actually ran into me, fleeing the crime, and still had the wit to invent a satisfactory story. I simply accepted your presence, and that of Brother Peter, the bursar, when he appeared soon after.'

'But why didn't you just accept that the clerk, Gryffin, had shot him accidentally with his bow?'

Falconer leaned against the balustrade of the stairwell to ease his tired legs.

'The angle of the arrow, and the position of the body. The arrow had pierced Sinibaldo in an upwards direction. Fired from outside in the courtyard, it would have been dipping. Then I saw a new gouge in the wood of a post in the kitchen. It was obviously where the arrow had struck. I couldn't make sense of this at first and pursued all sorts of silly ideas, thinking that the Bishop had been the intended victim. If only I had applied simple Aristotelean logic there and then, I would not have wasted so much time.'

Falconer shook his head at his own foolishness.

'Once I had eliminated all other possibilities, I found myself returning to the obvious, and the arrow. A hit on Sinibaldo from that distance, through an opened door and into a darkened room, would have been a truly miraculous shot. No, I realized the killer had taken advantage of this heaven-sent instrument of death to carry out his intended deed and cover his tracks. He had probably decided on murder anyway – the overturned pots suggested a struggle was already taking place. Then the arrow came through the doorway and struck the timbers in the room. Our killer simply pulled it free and thrust it upwards into Sinibaldo's heart. Of course, if the killer was acting at close quarters, then the intended victim must have been Sinibaldo all along. It could not have been a case of mistaken identity.

'And that meant the killer had to be you or Brother Peter. No one else was in the vicinity to seize the chance. I have to confess, I tended towards Brother Peter at first. I mean, he is so severe and you are so, well, jolly.'

A sad smile crossed Darby's strained features, but Falconer continued his exposition.

'I had seen him myself going to see Humphrey Segrim. So that suggested him as one of the conspirators. But then I learned from Mistress Segrim that he had simply gone to lend her husband money to sustain his farm. She also told me about your informing the Abbot of Brother Peter's trip to Wallingford on the day of John Gryffin's murder.'

The monk was puzzled.

'Why would that have made you suspicious of me? Surely it would have pushed you in the opposite direction.'

'It would have done, except I already knew where Brother Peter was on that day, all day, which meant he could not have been at Wallingford. So I had to ask myself why you were telling lies about him. And then today, I had all my suspicions confirmed.'

Falconer stepped over to the monk, took his hands, and raised them up to his face.

'I saw the hands of the person who strangled Segrim. They were covered in ink.'

John Darby's fingers were indeed stained with faint echoes of the reds, yellows and blues of the inks he so lovingly applied to his manuscripts. The monk's cherubic face contorted in a snarl.

'Sinibaldo truly had the mark of Cain upon him. He planned to kill his own brother, the Pope's appointed legate to England. It was an easy decision to assist in his death.'

Angrily, he shook Falconer's hands free of his.

Startled at this move, Falconer stepped back and almost sealed his fate. He realized he was at the head of the creaky staircase, and about to fall. Clutching at the newel post to recover his balance, he was in no position to defend himself from Darby's onslaught. Those fingers that worked so delicately on beautiful lettering hooked themselves round Falconer's throat, and forced him back over the stairwell. Darby intended either to strangle him or to cast him down the steep steps. Falconer's arm muscles crackled as he fought to hang on to the post. He could feel the line of the top step gouging into his back, the smooth cloth of his robe helping his opponent to slide him further towards the drop. For the second time that day, Falconer appeared to be staring at death, but this time it was his own.

Suddenly there was an inhuman crack and the monk's grip on Falconer's throat relaxed. He looked up to see Darby's dead eyes in the middle of his reddened face. The whole head lolled at an unusual angle. Over his shoulder loomed the serious visage of Guillaume de Beaujeu, his arm crooked around the monk's neck. He had snapped it as coldly and simply as if it were that of a chicken due for the pot.

He kept his arm around the monk and with the other gently assisted Falconer to his feet. As the Regent Master recovered his breath, de Beaujeu pressed his finger to his lips and slid the body down the stairs that were to have brought about Falconer's demise. They watched the body tumble to the bottom, then the Templar spoke.

'No one need ever know it was anything more than an unfortunate accident,' he explained, and led Falconer down the stairs before the scribes, responding to the strange noises, issued from the Scriptorium.

Chapter Sixteen

Falconer was happy to be back in the familiar surroundings of his own room at Aristotle's Hall. Some days had passed since the solemn burial of Brother John Darby in the peaceful cemetery at Oseney Abbey alongside the brethren who had passed to glory before him. There seemed no benefit from laying accusations of murder at the doors of the abbey, and his death was seen as a tragic accident. All the monks knew he would be sorely missed, and a new prior and master of copying would be difficult to find.

The Regent Master was celebrating the full recovery of his health, and had spent fourpence of his meagre income on a robust Gascon wine which he now opened in the company of Peter Bullock and the Templar Guillaume de Beaujeu. The latter was shortly to return to France, and Falconer was anxious to prise just a little more of the facts of the recent case from him.

After a while, they had all consumed sufficient of the wine to make the conversation free and ribald, even though the Frenchman had denigrated its simple qualities. He did not demur, however, when it came to refilling his tankard. Falconer had explained about the prediction of the eclipse in Friar Bacon's papers, and his idea to frighten Segrim into confession.

'I should have known his accomplice in the murders would not be so easily taken in.'

Bullock snorted with laughter, his wine slopping on to the floor.

'I don't know why he was not frightened. I knew what was afoot and Friar Fordam scared me to death.'

'And so you should have been, we all know whither you are bound at the Last Judgement.'

The comment delighted both Bullock and his drinking partners, and they toasted the constable's despatch to the sulphurous pit. Falconer still forebore from telling the man he had seen him as the face of God. That was something he could savour in private. Then Falconer turned to the Templar with a question.

'I assume that the Bishop's denial of his brother's complicity in an attempt on his life was incorrect. And that the conspiracy involving Segrim and Darby sought to despatch Sinibaldo before he despatched the Bishop, on whom so much of the King's plans depended.'

'Oh, indeed. Sinibaldo had tried several times to end his brother's life, the last in the King's own residence in London. Then it was by means of poison to be administered by a bogus doctor. Whether he did it out of pure jealousy or hope of advancement, who knows? I was instructed to enlist him, so that the Orsinis', and your King's, candidate for Pope was eliminated. But Sinibaldo was killed before I arrived, leaving me with the need to find out who had done it.'

'But why?' asked the constable. 'If your contact was dead, why did it matter who had carried out the deed?'

Falconer cut in before the Templar could reply for himself.

'Because, if you had discovered the Bishop was involved in the demise of his own brother, you could have used it to the same end. Eliminating Otho from the candidacy for Pope. By blackmail, if not by murder.'

De Beaujeu acknowledged Falconer's perspicacity with a slight inclination of his head.

'I must confess, though, I was not unhappy that he had been killed. I prefer to use an instrument that is a little more subtle than outright murder. Except where it is absolutely necessary. Then I use whatever means are at my disposal.'

'Like your own hands?'

De Beaujeu merely smiled his cold smile, and offered his tankard for more wine. Falconer poured and continued.

'Still, I should be grateful that you were at the abbey at the last. I had underestimated Darby, and the state of my recovery.'

He stopped pouring as a thought then occurred to him.

'Why were you there?'

Falconer saw an embarrassed look on Bullock's face, which he tried to mask with a deep draught from his tankard. But Falconer was not so easily diverted.

'You arranged for him to be there?'

'I could not let you beard the murderer in his den alone in the state you were in. But I knew it was not worth arguing with you about going there on your own. I also knew I could not follow you without you seeing me. But I remembered our Templar friend's stalking skills, having witnessed them. So I requested him to pick up your tracks as you left the postern gate and follow you. And a good job I did too, or you might have been at the foot of those stairs with a broken neck, not Brother John.'

Falconer swept aside the constable's annoyance at being found out with profuse thanks, and agreed he had saved him from his own foolishness. But still Bullock had a grumble about Falconer saving the worthless life of Humphrey Segrim. The Regent Master passed it off as unimportant.

'I doubt we shall hear of Segrim involving himself in affairs of state again. He is a humbled man. Mistress Ann told me yesterday he was paying more attention to his own affairs now. Apparently the manor needs some careful managing. He even asked her opinion on a money matter.'

'He certainly won't be able to shout at anyone for a long time yet,' chortled Bullock, putting his hands round his throat and making croaking noises by way of explanation. Having heard the story, de Beaujeu was curious about Falconer's revival of the apparently dead man.

'I have seen the same done with a drowned man in the Holy Land. It was a Jew did it then.'

'And it was from a Jew I learned the technique. It doesn't always work, however. This time I was lucky.'

He remembered how he had thought fleetingly of leaving Segrim dead. The vision of a widowed Ann Segrim had floated before his eyes, and the idea had been tempting. But only briefly. Anyway, he could never marry and retain his teaching benefice, and a wealthy widow would swiftly have attracted another husband. Better that Ann stayed married to a cowed Humphrey Segrim, who would have no more power to supervise his wife's every move. Falconer drove from his mind the possibilities that such a situation might present, and returned to wrapping up the loose ends of his tapestry of truths.

With an innocent look on his face, he leaned across the table towards de Beaujeu.

'What did you find out from John Gryffin when he was in Wallingford Castle's dungeon?'

De Beaujeu was too canny a person to be so easily caught out, and laughed at Falconer's attempted trap.

'You do not know whether I spoke to John Gryffin, or to anyone in Wallingford Castle. Yet you dare ask that? Well, as it no longer matters I will answer you. Yes, I did go to Wallingford.'

Bullock crashed his tankard down on the battered surface of the table, and snorted in satisfaction that his memory had not played him wrong. The Templar continued his story unperturbed.

'I had the good fortune to encounter a sleeping warden and relieved him easily of his keys. The boy was in a cell on his own, and so terrified of what was to happen to him, he would have done or said anything to escape. The poor lad thought incarceration was the worst thing that could occur. He didn't envisage death as his fate, and so soon at that. Anyway, he told me enough to convince me he had acted entirely on his own, and had not been involved in any plot.'

A wry smile crossed de Beaujeu's lips.

'He also said he just reacted out of anger and was amazed that his arrow had found its mark, as all his comrades derided his poor aim when it came to killing game. He said he had never hit anything in his life before, and couldn't see clearly from one side of his cell to the other. To hit a man at such a distance, he classed as a miracle.'

Falconer heard in poor Gryffin's words an echo of the words he had used with his killer only a few days before. The three men paused and pondered on the untimely and unfortunate death of a young man whose only crime had been accidentally to present a calculating murderer with his weapon of destruction. Bullock broke the silence with a question for his old friend.

'What I can't understand is why you were so worried about the potion Brother Talam was giving you, when I came in that day. To me it looked as though you thought he was poisoning you. Yet you say you never suspected him of being the murderer.'

Falconer chortled.

'True. By then I knew his innocence – and Darby's guilt, incidentally. You see, Ann Segrim came to me with some information she thought would be of great use. And it was, but not in the way she imagined. She overheard Darby telling Ralph Harbottle that Brother Talam had been to Wallingford on the fateful day. But I knew he couldn't have been, because I had already learned by chance that Talam was providing potions for Friar de Sotell's weak heart, and had ministered to him all that day after a particularly bad attack. He had provided him with a draught of foxglove extract, and sat with him. He didn't want anyone to know because there is no love lost between the Abbot and the Friar or, more precisely, their respective orders. I only found this out because I myself enquired after de Sotell's health.'

He waved his finger at the constable.

'Which only goes to show that all the facts are needed, no matter how insignificant or apparently unrelated, in order to find the truth about a murder.'

Bullock was not about to be diverted by the lecture, however. 'You still haven't told me why you feared Talam's potion.'

Falconer grinned sheepishly.

'I hate taking medicine, don't you?'

Epilogue

The events surrounding the death of the master of cooks of the Papal Legate are well recorded in history, as are the political consequences. For a time the gates of Oxford were closely watched and lectures suspended. Both excommunication and interdict were proclaimed on the University and town. However, several English bishops bluntly told the Papal Legate that his servants' attitude was much to blame. And after the offenders, less the unfortunate Gryffin, had taken part in a penitential procession through the streets of London, and paid for the repose of Sinibaldo's soul, a pardon was issued. Nowhere is it recorded who actually committed the murder, or why.

At this time Henry was forced by the barons of England to rid himself of most of his foreign advisers. But even this did not prevent matters simmering on until the barons' rebellion three years later. Bishop Otho left for Rome shortly after these events, which were described in several monastic chronicles, but failed in his bid to become Pope. James of Troyes, Patriarch of Jerusalem, was elected Pope on 29 August and took the name of Urban IV. In his turn, he died in 1265.

Guillaume de Beaujeu served the Order of the Poor Knights of the Temple well, and his path crossed that of William Falconer on other occasions. He eventually became its Grand Master in 1274.

Little is known of the rest of Humphrey Segrim's life, for while he was briefly associated in the chronicles with great names such as Aethelmar of Lusignan, there is no mention of him after the events of 1261. Similarly his wife is lost in safe and happy obscurity.

The *Chronica Oseneiensis* was kind to Ralph Harbottle and his pious and generous life is recorded in great detail, including the enhancement of the buildings at St John's Hospital. The bursar Peter Talam has a passing and grudgingly favourable mention also, though little is now known of their chronicler John Darby. The Dominicans too have little to say about Friar Robert Fordam, whose meteoric rise to celebrity with his prediction of the end of the world in 1261 or thereabouts was followed by a similarly swift descent into obscurity when the world carried on in its course. He is thought to have retired to a solitary cell in Northumbria, where he had no one to hypnotize but the gulls.

Thomas de Cantilupe served the University well as Chancellor, and eventually became Chancellor of England during the short-lived ascendancy of Baron Simon de Montfort. This, however, did not later prevent him from being a close adviser to de Montfort's conqueror, Edward I of England.

Peter Bullock died as he might have wished, as a warrior, in the midst of a pitched battle between northern and Welsh students. But not before he had been involved in many mysteries unravelled by his friend Regent Master Falconer.

William Falconer was to have many further adventures, occasioned by his insatiable curiosity. He travelled throughout England and abroad, finally making contact again with his life-long friend and mentor Friar Roger Bacon.